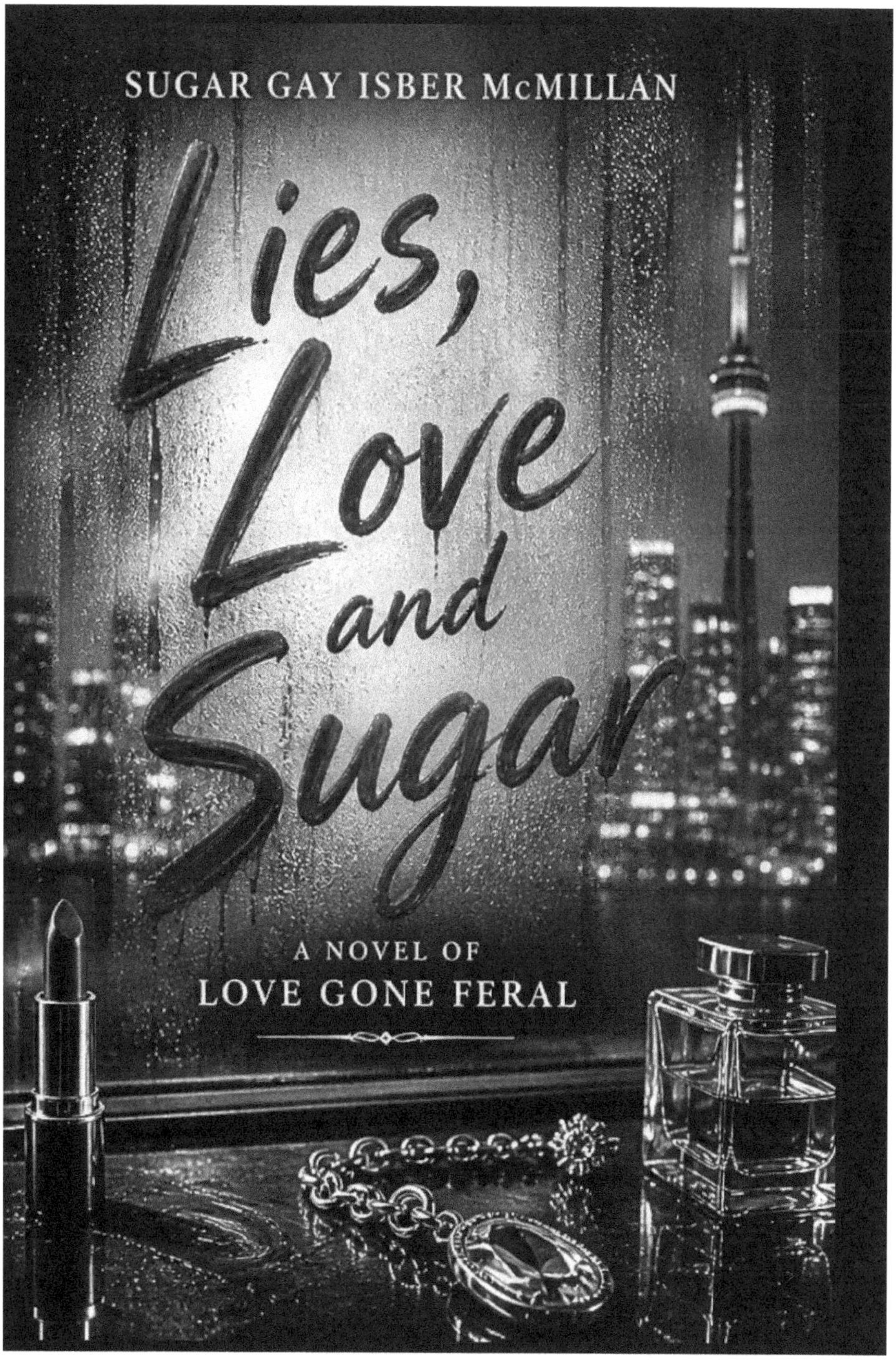

SUGAR GAY ISBER McMILLAN

Lies, Love and Sugar

A NOVEL OF
LOVE GONE FERAL

Published by The WOW Book Co.™
United States of America

ISBN: 978-1-967973-87-3

Cover design and interior design by the author.

First Edition

Lies, Love and Sugar

Lies, Love & *Sugar*

A Novel of Love Gone Feral

By

Sugar Gay Isber McMillan

Chapters

Love Gone Feral

I was not born feral.

I was made that way.

You don't wake up one morning snarling at shadows. You don't cross borders, tear up paperwork, throw logic to the wind because you're bored. Something has to break first. Something has to keep shifting until you no longer trust the ground beneath you.

Seamus Lee did not look dangerous.

That was the first trick.

He was trained to make people feel safe. That was his job. Undercover. Courtrooms. Confessions pulled from men who thought they were in control. He knew how to lean in without crowding. He knew how to lower his voice until you leaned closer. He knew how to look at you as if you were the only person in the room.

I thought that meant intimacy.

It meant skill.

He could sit across from a jury and hold them. He could sit across from a suspect and make them talk. He could sit across from me and let silence do the work.

He did not chase.
He positioned.

He did not confess.
He revealed in layers.

There was always just enough truth to make the lie believable.

I had loved before. I had married. I had survived illness and death and lawyers and the IRS breathing down my neck. I had crossed a border with two children and a suitcase full of china. I had stood in front of a queen and made her laugh.

I was not fragile.

But I had never loved a man trained to keep parts of himself sealed.

Undercover work requires compartments. Identities. Stories that are half-true and half-performance. It requires the ability to hold eye contact while withholding the center.

That skill does not turn off at home.

I did not know I was being calibrated.

When facts change slowly, you adjust.
When affection comes hot and then cold, you compensate.
When you are told you misunderstood, you try harder to understand.

You become vigilant.
You become suspicious.

You become someone who checks timelines and replays conversations in the dark.

You become feral.

Not because you are crazy.

Because your body knows something, but your heart is still negotiating.

There was the wife.
There was me.
And later, there was someone else.

Not an accident.
A pattern.

Wine and dine.
Charm and withdraw.
Return with an explanation just convincing enough to reset the clock.

He did not rage.
He managed.

And I unraveled in response.

That is the part people misunderstand.

They think feral means wild.

It doesn't.

Feral means you learned to survive without protection.

This is not the story of a woman who chased chaos.

It is the story of what happens when love is built on shifting ground, and the person shifting it has been professionally trained to do exactly that.

I had never been this version of myself before him.

After him, I would never be that woman again.

That was new.

And that is where this story begins.

TEXAS

Thank God I had a bra on when I walked through the room.

That was my first coherent thought after I realized my husband was dead.

The house was silent in a way that houses are never silent. Even grief makes noise. Refrigerators hum. Ice settles. Wood breathes. That morning, nothing moved.

When I called 9-1-1, I screamed so hard they thought I had shot him. Within minutes, the driveway was lined with police.

He died in our bed.

That horror is not this story.

But it is the doorway.

Because everything that followed began with that silence.

The Breaking Point

Death was clean compared to what came after.

Grief is private. Probate is public.

Within weeks, the quiet house filled with letters. Lawyers. Certified mail. Words like contest and claim and review. A simple will unraveled into something unrecognizable.

Family can turn angry when money enters the room. Even small money. Even the suggestion of money.

I hired one law firm. Then the other side would change law firms so it would start over. Then another. Rinse and repeat to slow the process and make me spend more money. Five in total, because each promised resolution and delivered only a delay. I was backed into a corner over and over.

The IRS circled. Deadlines stacked. Fees multiplied.

Three years went by.

Three years of holding my breath.

Three years of trying to keep two boys steady while everything underneath us shifted and they had no idea.

One afternoon, I learned something that split me open in a different way. My sons, both labeled gifted and talented, both accelerated, both tested and praised, were enrolled in one of the lowest-ranked schools in all of Texas.

I had been so busy surviving that I had missed the ground beneath them.

That was the moment I understood: staying was not stability.

It was stagnation.

A friend once looked at me during that period and said, "I don't know if you can take one more thing."

She was wrong.

I just could not stay.

CANADA

The Hurricane

I crossed a border because staying still would have destroyed us.

Long before I stood at that final bend in a rose garden, I stood in a basement laundry room in Ontario, staring at foam core and thinking, I cannot go backward.

After the Queen laughed and the cameras packed up and the roses were swept clean of the crowd, I drove home and remembered something.

I had not always known how to stand at the edge of a walkabout and call out to power.

There was a time I stood at the edge of a frozen balcony in Ontario with bottles of food coloring and every plastic container I owned.

The first winter I arrived in Canada, the snow did not feel hostile. It felt like a blank page.

I did not have work papers yet. I was not allowed to earn money. I was a newly married woman in a new country with two boys and a mathematician husband who had no idea he had married weather.

So, I made weather.

Every bowl, every Rubbermaid tub, every stray cup became a mold. I poured water and drops of red, blue, yellow. I lined them along the railing. I stacked them on the steps. I turned Coca-Cola bottles into frozen columns. I discovered that in Ontario, the world would hold whatever shape you gave it.

By morning, our balcony looked like a jewelry box overturned into the snow.

Blue bricks. Lemon cylinders. Scarlet spheres. Ice like cut gemstones.

My husband did not understand it. My boys did. I was an artist.

Later, in Waterloo, I carried that same idea to a winter dog festival. I dumped colored ice into a public square and told children to build. They stacked it like Lego. They knocked it down. They squealed when their mittens turned pink and turquoise.

The organizers put it on the cover of their magazine.

They called it innovative.

I called it survival.

Because three months into that marriage, I already knew it would not last.

So, I went downstairs into the basement laundry room, bought foam core from Michael's, and began painting hurricanes.

Big canvases. Thick strokes. Swirling color that looked like wind maps. My world was unstable. So I painted movement.

The bracelets came later.

A little box of beads from Pasadena. Fencing wire. One accidental bracelet.

Women at the art show grabbed my wrist and asked where they could buy it.

I had gone to sell paintings. I went home a jeweler.

I had crossed a border with two boys, a trunk full of Rosenthal china, and the kind of optimism that only appears after everything has fallen apart.

The marriage had happened in a week.
The paperwork had not.
I was not allowed to work.

So, I painted.

The laundry room had no carpet. That was its greatest virtue. I bought the largest foam core sheets Michael's would sell me because they were cheap and forgiving. I squeezed color onto plastic plates and dragged it across white surfaces until the canvases looked like weather systems.

Hurricanes. Every one of them.

My life felt exactly like that. Spinning. Loud. Uncertain where it would land. I had already discovered that the man I had married was still prowling the same dating website where we met, pretending to be someone else. I could not return to Texas. I could not stay still. So, I made art that moved.

The paintings were enormous. Juicy. Defiant. They said, "I am still here."

And then one afternoon, digging through a small box of beads I had hauled up from Pasadena, Texas without knowing why, I wrapped fencing wire around my wrist and made a bracelet.

I wore it to an international art show in Toronto, where I was showing my artworks.

People did not ask about the hurricanes.

They grabbed my arm.

"Where did you get that?"

That is how it started.

Not with a business plan.
Not with a strategy.
With a bracelet made in exile.

The next year, I returned to the same show with a vintage suitcase I had painted and lined like a treasure chest. The bracelets stood upright inside it, rows of color like sugared candy. Women leaned in. Men leaned in. Everyone wanted something they could carry away.

Jewelry was portable joy.

Paintings required wall space and courage. Bracelets required only a wrist.

I did not yet know that those wrists would one day include a queen's.

But I understood this: when your life is chaos, you build something you can hold.

Teaching My Audi TT to sing Italian

The first time I felt Canada, it was not in a courtroom or a customs office.

It was in an Audi TT with the top down.

The leather smelled expensive and hopeful. The seats were heated. The air was sharp enough to taste. Griffin sat beside me, bundled but grinning, and Andrea Bocelli poured out of the speakers like we had hired him for the ride.

I always told him I taught a German car how to sing Italian.

We sang every word we knew. Loud. Off key. Perfect.

The snow that night did not fall. It glittered. I had never seen snow sparkle like that. It caught the headlights and shattered into diamonds across the road. We were hunting for the northern lights. We had heard there was a chance. Neither of us had ever seen them. We did not even know what to look for. But we believed in the possibility.

We crested a hill and the world shifted.

Coming toward us in the opposite lane was a black horse at full gallop, pulling a Mennonite buggy. Steam poured from its nostrils in white bursts. The harness straps flashed in the headlights. The driver sat upright, steady, old world calm against our modern blur.

German engineering. Italian opera. A nineteenth century silhouette charging through the night.

I was not afraid.

I was alive.

We passed each other in our separate lanes, two different centuries acknowledging one another in the cold Ontario dark. The stars were ruthless and clear above us. The road felt endless. It was not. Later, when I traced the path on a map, I realized we had barely gone fifteen miles.

But that night felt enormous.

I had crossed a country.

I had crossed a life.

Cast Away

The truth is, Canada did not begin with glittering snow.

It began with a storm.

When I first arrived, the Blue Water Bridge had been swallowed by a snow dump so heavy they closed it to cars. I did not own boots. I did not own gloves worthy of a Canadian winter. I owned Texas confidence and two boys.

We walked across that bridge in a blizzard.

I remember thinking that this felt symbolic but I did not yet know of what.

Customs was not romantic. Paperwork never is. But that is where the pivot happened. I was no longer just a widow tangled in litigation. I was an immigrant in motion.

That same day, we sat in a McDonald's in Sarnia, and I could not decide what to order. I had barely eaten fast food in years. The menu was a wall of choices I did not understand. He grew impatient. His voice sharpened. He yelled and sulked and became a monster. His mother lowered her eyes in quiet apology.

That was the first crack.

Later that day, we went to see Cast Away. The opening scene was Texas. I was sitting in Canada, wrapped in snow, watching my old state flicker across a movie screen.

His mother leaned toward me and whispered, "Look at that. You're here, but you're still there."

She was small and elegant and kind. When she died years later, they buried her wearing a pin I had made from fencing wire and beads. Even after the marriage dissolved, she kept my jewelry close.

Some loves remain.

Rainbow Ice

Three months into the marriage, I understood something quietly and completely.

This was not my forever.

There was no screaming revelation. No dramatic confession. Just a slow clarity that the man I had crossed a border for was living in a different interior world than I was. He moved through rooms like a mathematician solving invisible equations. I moved through rooms like someone rearranging light.

We were mismatched frequencies.

So I went downstairs.

The basement became mine.

If I could not fix a marriage, I could make something beautiful.

The snow that winter was relentless. It piled against the balcony rails, pressed against the steps, swallowed the yard. Most people saw inconvenience. I saw material.

I began freezing color.

Every container in the house became a mold. Buckets. Rubbermaid tubs. Bowls. Anything that would hold water. I mixed food coloring into it, dropped in beads, petals, bits of ribbon, fragments of things. I slid trays onto the balcony and watched them harden overnight.

By morning the railing was lined with jewels.

Amber blocks. Sapphire slabs. Ruby circles. Ice that caught the winter light and fractured it into prisms. I stacked them along the fencing, lined the steps, built temporary installations that glowed for a few hours each day before the sun softened their edges.

He had no idea what to do with this.

He had never seen someone leave Coca Cola in a snowbank on purpose because nature was a better refrigerator. He had never seen someone treat a blizzard like an art supply shipment.

He was numbers.

I was color.

The boys understood immediately. They helped carry buckets. They suggested new shades. We would wake up and run outside to see what had frozen perfectly and what had cracked in the night.

The marriage was cooling.
The balcony was radiant.

And then one day, he was gone.
And I was not.

The Bracelet That Would Not Behave

The marriage ended quietly.

No explosion. No cinematic exit. Just a slow awareness that I was living beside someone who could not see me. When he left, he did it efficiently. He always did everything efficiently. Mathematics is tidy. Life is not.

The house felt larger after that. Not emptier. Larger.

I started hosting jewelry parties because I needed to pay bills and because I liked the sound of women laughing around a table. I would set out bowls of beads like candy dishes. Czech fire-polished crystals. Vintage glass from Germany. Old chain I'd hunted down online at two in the morning. I didn't think of myself as a jeweler. I thought of myself as someone rearranging light.

At one Christmas party, I made a bracelet that looked like it had been plugged into the wall.

Faceted red. Deep evergreen. Twilight blue. Champagne gold. When the chandelier hit it, it flashed like a string of lights wrapped around a tree.

A friend borrowed it for the holidays. She wore it to events all over Ontario. Charity dinners. Store openings. Winter galas where people stood near tall windows and talked about snow and politics and who was moving where.

That bracelet traveled farther than I did.

I started hearing about it.

"Who made that?"
"Where did you get it?"
"Is she local?"

The CN Tower gift shop manager was at one of those events. She watched the bracelet move through conversations like it had its own orbit. She didn't ask for my number. She asked for a meeting.

The Ghost with The Yellow Rose

Around that same time, I invited my gal pals to come for wine and the future. I had been told about a local woman who had the gift and she was available to come for a fair price. I was so excited.

Not because I was lost. Because I was curious.

I created a space for her that was away from the chatter with a table and comfortable chairs.

My friends had their turns and I waited until the group paused and I went in.

She took my hands and went very quiet.

The psychic held my hands longer than necessary.

Her eyes moved slightly to the left as if she were watching something over my shoulder.

"I see someone who passed," she said softly. "A man smoking a cigar. He says he was your husband."

I froze.

It was not a chapter I carried lightly. His absence had weight. Not drama. Weight.

She squeezed my fingers.

"He's not worried," she said. "He's proud."

That was unexpected.

Then she tilted her head.

"And I see a yellow rose. It keeps showing up. I don't know if that means anything to you."

It didn't. Not yet.

Yellow rose. Texas? Friendship? Warning? I had no idea. But she said it twice.

"You'll know when it's time."

Then she leaned back.

"He says he is giving you the yellow rose for your birthday."

I laughed.

The Call

The CN Tower gift shop manager called a week later.

"I've seen your bracelet," she said. "Bring everything."

Everything?

I packed my dining room into plastic bins. Bracelets, pins, earrings. Fire-polished Czech crystals in red, green, blue. Vintage German glass. Wire twisted into organic shapes that felt like something growing instead of something manufactured. I did not walk into the CN Tower meeting with samples.

I walked in with history.

Seven tractor-trailers of history.

A man in New York had owned a bead and findings store on Fifth Avenue through the height of American costume jewelry. The sixties. The seventies. The Rhode Island factories humming. When he died, what remained wasn't inventory. It was time.

New old stock (NOS).

Unopened cartons. Vintage German glass. Czech fire polished crystals. Brass stampings never assembled. Components that had waited decades for hands. Yellowed paper that crumbled if you touched it with vintage pearls stashed inside, as that gleamed on delicate strings.

I found them the way prospectors find veins of gold. eBay at midnight. Auctions closing at 2:17 a.m. I bought from the family in West Virginia, piece by piece, until they knew my name. I even drove to visit them. They visited me. I carried history home in flat-rate boxes.

I tried not to use modern crystal at first. I wanted story, not sparkle for sparkle's sake. I wanted bracelets that felt like they had already lived a life before they reached your wrist.

When I laid my pieces out on that beige conference table at the CN Tower, the fluorescent lighting did not deserve them.

Red like lacquered ornaments.
Green like cathedral glass.
Blue like the edge of winter dusk.
Gold catching like candle flame.

The manager didn't negotiate.

"We'll take it."

"All of it."

Every bracelet. Every pin. Every pair of earrings.

When I packed up, my case was empty.

Completely empty.

For a moment, I didn't move.

All of it.

It felt like someone had opened a window in a room I didn't know was airless.

I walked out of that meeting into the Toronto sunlight and felt something inside me lift. I wanted to throw my hat into the air like Mary Tyler Moore and spin in a circle on Front Street.

I walked out of that building lighter than air, carrying nothing but a hollow case and a pulse I could feel in my throat.

My phone was dead.

Of course it was.

This was before chargers lived in cars. Before battery percentages ruled our lives. My little Motorola had given up sometime during the meeting. I couldn't call my crew back in Waterloo. I couldn't tell anyone.

Instead, I walked.

Straight into the future.

Coffee Near the Sky

I had a meeting afterward.

Not about jewelry.

About curiosity.

We had matched on a dating app. That still makes me laugh. Algorithms doing what fate used to handle.

He was already seated when I walked into the coffee shop near the Tower.

Cowboy boots under the table. Real ones, not costume.
Silver hair, long enough to curl at the collar.
A goatee that hid his smile until it surprised you.
Blue eyes that assessed and amused at the same time.

Barrel-chested. Well-tailored jacket. The kind of man who smells faintly of clean soap and the ghost of a cigar from the night before.

He stood when I approached.

"You look like you just robbed a bank," he said.

"I just sold one," I answered.

That twinkle. That belly chuckle. That was the thing about him. He carried bravado, yes, but it was wrapped in humor. A businessman. An attorney. Former undercover cop. A man who had lived several lives already and looked like he might live three more.

I told him about the Tower.

About the table.

About the fact that they bought everything.

He leaned back and studied me.

"That's scale," he said. "You don't think small."

We talked longer than I meant to.

Retail. Risk. Reinvention. How a city rewards nerve.

At one point, he said, "Let me take you to dinner."

I shook my head.

"I have to drive home."

I did not need to be carried anywhere that day. I had already climbed something.

He walked me to the door.

There was snow in the air again. Light, almost decorative.

"I'll call you," he said.

"You can," I replied.

And I left with the biggest grin on my face.

The Silence on the Highway

I drove the hour and a half home, vibrating with news I had to carry alone.

The silence on the highway felt holy.

The sky was low and winter-blue. My empty case lay open on the passenger seat like proof. I kept glancing at it as if it might rcfill itself.

By the time I reached Waterloo, my phone was still dead. No way to tell anyone. No way to celebrate out loud.

It felt almost sacred to hold that kind of victory privately.

The next morning, my phone rang.

R.

His voice had a smile in it.

"So," he said, "did you come back down to earth?"

"I don't plan to," I answered.

We fell into it easily. Not flirtation. Not yet. Sparring.

He liked that I didn't defer. I liked that he didn't intimidate.

By the end of the call, he had invited himself to Waterloo.

The First Night in Waterloo

He arrived in a black Suburban.

Suit pressed. Boots polished. Silver hair catching the last of the light. That curl at the collar. The goatee hid most of his mouth, so you had to watch his eyes to know when he was amused.

He was always amused.

"You ready?" he asked.

"For what?"

"To be properly taken out."

No one had said that to me in years.

He found a restaurant downtown that I had never tried. White tablecloths. Low lighting. The kind of place where wine lists are presented like sacred texts.

He ordered confidently. He always did.

We talked through appetizers. Through the main course. Through dessert. The kind of conversation where you don't check the time because time has checked out.

He told me about working undercover. About walking into rooms where no one knew who he really was. About the moment he decided to become an attorney, because he wanted control of the narrative instead of just proximity to it.

I told him about beads that were older than we were. About buying history in cardboard boxes. About turning dining rooms into studios.

His phone buzzed more than once.

He glanced at it, ignored it.

"There's always someone looking for me," he said lightly.

There was bravado there. But there was also truth.

At some point, over a glass of wine that tasted like velvet, he said it casually.

"I have children."

I looked at him.

"Three grown. And one younger."

"Younger how?"

"Fifteen."

He said it without shame. Without apology. Like it was simply architecture.

"And their mother?" I asked.

"We're… complicated."

Of course they were.

He spoke about the youngest with something close to awe. The surprise of her. The joy of her. The way his wife had agreed to absorb the reality of another child.

It was a red flag dressed as honesty.

I saw it.

I did not walk away.

Because by then the restaurant had emptied and we were the last ones left, chairs turned upside down around us, waitstaff hovering politely.

We closed the place down.

Outside, the air was cold and sharp. He put his hand at the small of my back as we walked to the car.

That small touch was electric.

Back at my house, there was that suspended moment at the door. The one where you could still choose differently.

He leaned in slowly. Not rushed. Not greedy.

The kiss felt like something I had been waiting for without knowing I was waiting.

The rest of the night unfolded the way nights do when two people are equally matched in humor and hunger and timing.

We didn't sleep much.

Before dawn, he was already dressed.

He liked to leave early. He liked to arrive early. A man always in motion.

By the time I woke properly, my phone was ringing again.

“Already miss me?” he asked.

He was halfway back to Toronto.

And I was already hooked.

A Man Who Lived in Motion

After that first night, we didn't cool down.

We accelerated.

Texts. Calls. Voice messages. Midday jokes. Late-night check-ins. We were both talkers, and neither of us wanted the line to go quiet.

He loved stories. Especially his own.

Undercover narcotics. Months at a time embedded. False identities. Wire taps. Warehouses. Long games. The kind of operations you only see in films, except his stories didn't have background music. They had paperwork and exhaustion and adrenaline.

He'd worked big cases. International ones. He'd been in Texas during Waco. He knew the underbelly of cities I had only known as skylines.

He spoke about it like a man who had seen everything and survived it.

His phone rang constantly.

Middle of the night, he'd wake, answer in a low voice, solve something in under three minutes, and roll back into sleep like a switch had flipped.

He was now the attorney cops called when things went sideways. He knew their language. He knew their fear.

He knew how to navigate systems because he had lived inside them.

There was bravado, yes.

But there was also competence.

He called it being "zoomed."

To zoom someone was to catch them off guard. To outplay them. To surprise them so cleverly they had to admire you for it.

He loved a good zoom story.

And I listened.

The Weekend Away

Two weeks in, he suggested a weekend.

Not a casual one.

A Relais & Châteaux country estate converted from an old mansion. Michelin-star kitchen. Rooms so few and so pristine you felt like you'd been admitted to something secret.

He sent red roses ahead of time.

My girlfriends were chattering with delight.

"Who is this man?"
"Are you serious?"
"Sugar, you've hooked a big one."

I didn't argue.

I arrived early.

The room had white linens so immaculate they almost shimmered. A small fireplace. A soaking tub the size of a confession booth. Thick drapes. Silver trays. The kind of bathroom fixtures that make you stand a little straighter.

I scattered the red roses across the bed.

Dramatic? Absolutely.

I ran a bath. Took my time. Dressed carefully. Jewelry, of course. Always jewelry.

When he walked in, he stopped.

"Now that," he said softly, "is an entrance."

We had been building toward that weekend all week. The calls had grown warmer. The teasing more pointed. The pauses longer.

Dinner downstairs was slow and indulgent. Courses arriving like choreography. Wine deep and dangerous.

We closed that restaurant too.

Back in the room, the roses were still fresh. Too fresh.

White sheets. Red petals. Heat. Laughter. The kind of closeness that makes you forget which side of the bed you started on.

In the morning, those immaculate sheets looked like a crime scene from a romance novel.

Petals crushed. Juice everywhere. Scarlet smears across pristine linen. It looked like a bloody crime scene.

We laughed about it.

And then I waited.

The Zoom

Two days later, one of my friends called him.

She introduced herself in a clipped, professional voice as legal counsel for the estate hotel.

There had been damage. Rolling around on red rose petals looked like a battle had happened on them.

The sheets, she explained, retailed at twelve hundred dollars.

There was silence.

He knew those sheets had not survived.

He began calculating. Legal angles. Liability. Tone.

"Finally", she said, " Sugar just zoomed you."

Dead silence.

Then an explosion of laughter.

He called me immediately.

"You got me large," he said, still laughing. "Large."

He was impressed.

That mattered.

He loved that I played back.

He loved that I didn't just receive the story. I wrote one.

The Hook

By then, I was in.

Not because he dazzled me with hotels.

Not because of the roses.

Because he met me in speed. In humor. In nerve.

He was motion.

And I had just learned how to climb.

We fit in that velocity.

He couldn't see me the next weekend.

Visitation.

Taylor.

There was something grounding about that. He wasn't just velocity. He was also a father on schedule.

We talked anyway. Texted. Laughed. Built anticipation like architects.

By the time we planned the next weekend, it wasn't dinner.

It was a motorcycle.

"Bring something you can ride in," he said.

My girlfriend dragged me shopping.

"Men are visual," she told me. "And this one? He rides."

Black jeans. Tank. Leather jacket. Boots. Jewelry that wouldn't catch in the wind.

I stood in front of the mirror and didn't recognize the woman looking back.

She looked like she was about to get on the back of something powerful.

And she was.

The Week Without Him

He couldn't see me the next weekend.
Visitation.

He said it casually. "Taylor weekend."

And I surprised myself by not being annoyed.
I liked that he showed up for his daughter.

Instead, we filled the hours with calls. Long ones. Midnight ones. Quick ones between meetings. The kind where you hang up and immediately replay the last joke.

He told me more about undercover work. Months at a time, pretending to be someone else. Living inside lies to get at the truth. Watching men crumble over money and powder. Listening for weakness.

"I was good at it," he said, not bragging. Just stating a fact.

He had been sent south once, he told me. Big cases. Dangerous rooms. He described the way a room changes temperature when a deal is about to go bad.

His phone buzzed constantly while we talked. Even on the weekends he had Taylor, it never fully stopped. Officers in trouble. Old colleagues. People who trusted him.

"You're dating a very busy man," he teased.

"I prefer a man in demand," I said back.

That was us. Constant volley.

He loved the word zoom.
Loved the art of catching someone off balance.
Loved the story of it after.

So, I zoomed him as often as possible, keeping him off balance and showing him I was his equal.

And the laugh that came out of him when he realized I had? That laugh did something to me.

It wasn't just an attraction anymore.

It was a partnership and a new love addiction.

The Shaky Bridge

In one of our late-night phone calls, when the conversation had softened and stretched into that velvety hour where voices lower without noticing, he said it.

"Let me show you Ontario. The Ontario I love."

I was done for.

I had explored on my own before. Drove north. Drove west. Wandered through small towns and along frozen lakes. But this was different. This would be on the back of a Harley. Or in that black Suburban that looked like it had seen things and survived them.

He told me to meet him near the 404 and the 400. We would head toward Barrie, toward Lake Simcoe.

"You bring a picnic," he said. "I'll do the driving."

The practical meeting point? A police station.

My car would be safe there, he assured me. And I could tell he liked pulling in like that. He liked being known. Liked the nods. Liked the subtle display.

I cooked like I was auditioning for a show about Man Food.

Barbecued ribs. Marinated mozzarella. Italian delicacies from a tiny shop that smelled like garlic and money. A proper meal. Dessert was tucked carefully in a container. We would buy wine and whiskey along the way.

When I climbed onto the back of his bike and wrapped my arms around his chest, the world rearranged itself.

The wind. The vibration. His hand briefly covering mine. The casual strength of him handling the machine. He talked over his shoulder about bikes he'd owned, highways he'd conquered, deals he'd survived.

Then he said it.

"Let's find the perfect place."

"For a picnic?" I shouted.

"Not exactly, a bit more."

He got off the freeway. Back roads. Gravel dust. Sun high and shameless.

"Let's look for land," he said. "Something for sale. No houses. Water if we're lucky."

"You're suggesting we trespass?"

"I'm suggesting we live large a little."

He was a criminal attorney. Former undercover cop. And here he was, coaxing me onto private land in broad daylight.

I said yes.

Not because he pushed.

Because I understood something.

During the week before that ride, I had been researching. How to hook a man. How to create memory. How to become unforgettable.

And I discovered the shaky bridge theory.

Anyone can walk across a normal bridge. It's forgettable. But a bridge that sways? That makes your pulse spike? That demands focus?

That's the one you remember.

I decided I would not be safe. I would be electric.

We found a wide stretch of land with a For Sale sign leaning slightly sideways. A stream cut through the back. No house in sight. Just sky and possibility.

We parked.

We carried the blanket.

We carried the wine.

We carried danger.

There is something about risk that sharpens everything. The taste of food. The brush of skin. The sound of laughter.

I wasn't just along for the ride.

I was creating it.

I matched his story for story. Tease for tease. I did not blush. I did not shrink. I did not follow.

I met him.

And when we rode back that afternoon, sunburned and grinning and absolutely certain we'd gotten away with something, I knew the game had shifted.

He called me the minute he hit his apartment in Toronto.

"You're trouble," he said.

"Zoomed?" I asked.

"Zoomed large."

The following week, he asked me to ride with him to Oshawa. A courthouse morning. A lakeside afternoon.

That became our rhythm.

Courthouse steps. White shirt under leather. Helmet hair and briefcase. Then lake roads and stolen afternoons.

I would watch him transform. From attorney in polished boots to man in denim and wind.

We weren't just sleeping together.

We were accelerating.

And acceleration is intoxicating.

I learned what made him laugh. What made him quiet. What made him lean closer. I learned how to keep him slightly off balance.

Not needy.

Not available.

But thrilling.

There's a difference.

And I could feel it.

He was no longer leading the ride.

We were.

I didn't realize I already had the power. He just had the charisma.

The Building

Somewhere between courthouse rides and stolen lake afternoons, I realized something.

Sex was powerful.

Chemistry was intoxicating.

But it was not permanent.

If I wanted to stand beside him and not underneath him, I needed something more than heat.

I needed gravity.

I told myself I was ready. That I had always been ready. But if I am honest, the urgency was sharpened by him. I wanted him to look at me and feel proud. Not just possessive. Proud.

But the shaky bridge theory had rewired me.

If I wanted to be unforgettable, I needed to build something that shook the ground.

I never liked hair salons. I cut my own hair. Colored it myself. I hated sitting in a chair under fluorescent lights while strangers inspected my head.

But one of my girlfriends had stunning hair. She gave me the name of a place.

"Go," she said. "You'll love it."

I didn't love it.

But I wanted to look extraordinary.

I left early. The salon wasn't far. For no particular reason, I turned down a side street instead of taking the main road. I've always done that. I like seeing the backs of things. The hidden angles. The way a city really lives.

I was two blocks from the salon when traffic stopped.

Police. A wrecker. A car twisted at an impossible angle. It had blown through a four-way stop and plowed into a metal roll-up garage door of the building on the corner. Not even at the corner, oddly. It had driven straight into the side.

It had just happened. I could feel that.

Then a train started crossing behind the building. A long one. I was boxed in. Cars behind me. No exit.

So, I turned off the engine and waited.

And I looked up.

Red brick.

Not timid red. Deep red. Confident red.

Green industrial window frames arched high across the façade. Massive windows. The kind you don't see anymore. The kind that belong to another era when buildings were meant to last longer than their owners.

The garage door was dented from the crash, metal caved in like a punched tin can. But the brick had barely flinched.

Three courses thick, I would later learn.

Built like it expected war.

There was a For Sale sign in the window.

I did not mean to fall in love.

But I did.

It was masculine and feminine at once. Solid but luminous. Abandoned but defiant. The kind of building that had survived decades without asking permission.

I picked up my phone before I consciously decided to.

I dialed.

When the agent answered, I said, "The price just went down. Someone drove into your building."

Silence on the other end.

"I'm nearby," he said finally.

"I'm getting my hair done," I replied calmly. "Go take a look. We'll talk."

I sat in that salon chair, uncomfortable as ever, while someone painted my hair. And all I could see was red brick and green arches.

I didn't care about highlights.

I cared about square footage and my hair still did not suit me.

The next day, I walked inside.

It was a wreck.

Tools left behind. Oil stains. Dust layered thick. The former mechanic had cleared out, but not gracefully.

And yet.

The light.

Those windows flooded the first floor like a cathedral of industry. The second floor was darker, punctured by old portals where massive insulators once connected the city's electricity to the grid. Birds had claimed a few openings. Air moved freely.

It had been a 1920s hydro switching station. Electricity from Niagara Falls would flow in and distribute outward. It had powered neighborhoods and the city of Kitchener, Ontario.

Now it sat hollow, waiting.

The agent never mentioned that he owned it himself. That omission should have warned me.

It didn't.

I walked the perimeter. Touched the brick. Counted the windows.

And I saw it.

A studio.

A loft.

A life.

Not dependent on anyone's last name.

Not waiting for anyone's permission.

"I'll buy it," I said.

I was off to the races.

Owning Brick

Once I said yes to the building, there was no turning back.

But owning brick meant sacrificing comfort.

I had a house I loved. A big one. I had redone every inch of it. My son Griffin was in the basement, drifting a little too long. It was just the two of us rattling around in all that square footage, plus the steady parade of workers and projects that followed me wherever I lived.

At the time, I was in the middle of a massive job for Procter & Gamble. Nine thousand necklaces in five weeks for a CoverGirl promotion. Three dollars apiece. It sounds small until you multiply it. I needed every dollar.

If I wanted that building, I had to sell the house.

I had to move my son forward.

I had to gamble.

Seamus was calling, but I didn't tell him right away. That was deliberate.

Mystery is a form of power.

I signed the papers. I toured the building with my girlfriends. They stared at the broken windows and peeling paint and shook their heads.

"You're insane."

They loved me. They supported me. But they could not see it.

I could.

The brick was not ruined. It was waiting.

When Seamus said he'd be in the area, I told him to meet me at an address. No explanation.

He showed up.

He looked at the derelict red brick structure, the dented garage door, the broken glass.

"Why are we here?"

I smiled.

"Maybe not today," I said, "but someday we're going to make love in this building."

He laughed.

Then I added, casually, "It's mine."

Silence.

That was the zoom.

Not a prank. Not a tease.

Ownership.

I walked him through like it was already a palace. I described the chandeliers. The glass doors. The studio downstairs. The loft upstairs. The way light would flood the first floor like a cathedral of creation.

I was vibrating.

He took me to dinner that night. We drank wine. We ended back at my house, tangled together, but the real intimacy wasn't in the sheets.

It was in the fact that I had just bought a future.

He encouraged me. Smiled. Said it would be beautiful.

He had no idea how beautiful.

Building the Diamond

I decided to sell the house and buy the building outright. No mortgage. No dependence. Cash in hand meant control. I closed on the sale of my house on my birthday, in June.

Six months. That was my deadline. Opening right after Christmas. Opening before Christmas would have been better, but it was not possible.

The space was gutted. Oil-stained floors. Bird access upstairs. Electrical ghosts from the 1920s still haunting the walls.

I called a Polish handyman I'd worked with before. Skilled. Practical. Honest.

He walked through shaking his head.

"This is big."

"I know," I said. "We're going to make it grand."

Downstairs would be open and bright. Jewelry displays. Long tables for classes. An event kitchen. Space for children to learn. Art on the walls. Light everywhere.

The crushed metal garage door would become a glass entrance.

Upstairs would be home. Heated bathroom floors. Granite rescued from a monument yard in steel blues and cool grays. A large animal water trough turned bathtub and walls wrapped in corrugated tin. This was Texas chic which had not found it's way to Canada yet. I added sliding glass doors instead of ordinary ones so everything glowed instead when closed.

Three massive chandeliers over the dining table because if light was an issue, I would create more of it. It acted as a room divider hanging from the ceiling.

The Italian furniture I ordered from Houston arrived like royalty. Blonde wood with delicate woven pattern inlays. A tiger Ultrasuede vavoom sofa. A glass table that could extend into a banquet. Vintage chrome swivel chairs with wheels, I had recovered in a velvet leopard print. Oriental rugs layered like stories.

All new artworks I painted in vibrant, bold reds against soft vintage green walls.

The building began to breathe.

And then there was the part no one talks about.

I went to the soup kitchen.

I hired men who needed work. Paid them daily in cash plus fed them breakfast and lunch and drove them back in time for dinner.

They had skills. Real ones. Carpentry. Framing. Tiling. Problem-solving.

They blossomed.

So did I.

I hauled materials in the back of my Saturn. Home Depot knew my name. I measured, planned, coordinated. Sheetrock, 2 x 4 building timbers, and plywood deliveries were the only indulgences that would not fit in my car.

The city tried to slow me down. Required plans. Permits. Inspections.

Fine.

I hired an architect to draft what I had already envisioned. The plans were simply a translation of what was in my head.

Later, I would learn that some people at City Hall had quietly bet I would never finish.

They didn't know me.

Six months later, I opened.

And it was magnificent.

The Shaky Bridge Revealed

Seamus would drop by in boots and denim, look around at the progress, and whistle softly.

"Let's get away this weekend," he'd say.

And I would hesitate.

Because for the first time, I was choosing between a man and a masterpiece.

I chose both.

But the building always won.

My goal had been simple. I wanted him proud. I wanted him to see me not as the woman on the back of his bike, but as an equal force.

I had built something that could outlast us.

That was the real zoom.

The First Crack

Ontario became our playground.

Courthouse to courthouse. Oshawa. Kawarthas. Port Perry. Small towns that existed only because a judge had once decided they should.

He loved food the way other men love trophies. Every town had a restaurant he swore by. Italian places wherc the red sauce tasted like someone's grandmother was still alive in the kitchen. Greek tavernas with lamb that fell off the bone. Tiny delis tucked beside courthouses where he would nod at the owner like they shared secrets.

"Best in the province," he'd say.

And it always was.

Sometimes it was not about court at all.

"Let's go to the nudist resort," he'd grin. "Just for the pool."

And I would pack a picnic that looked like it belonged in a Dutch still-life. Grapes. Cheese. Ribs. Wine decanted into something more civilized than the bottle. Paper plates, yes. But arranged like porcelain.

We were absurd and magnificent.

Going home from those trips meant returning to my project. At that point I wasn't even sleeping in the building yet. I was staying in a friend's vacant house, stripped of furniture because she was trying to sell it empty. I slept on an air mattress. Every morning I deflated it and hid the evidence of my existence so that showings could happen without revealing I was there.

I paid rent.

She charged me.

I remember thinking that was an odd kind of loyalty.

Seamus, meanwhile, would happily pay for a hotel when we met somewhere along his route. Neutral territory. Easy exits.

And then one evening, in the quiet after we had exhausted ourselves and the air between us was still warm and heavy, I asked him.

"Tell me about your divorce."

He didn't flinch.

"I'm not divorced."

The words landed softly. Too softly.

I pulled back just enough to look at him.

"I'm not dating someone who isn't divorced."

He squeezed my hand. That steady, confident squeeze.

"I'll get a divorce," he said. "I'll get one."

He was already living separately. He had his own apartment. His wife, he explained, didn't drive. It frightened her. She relied on him. On the children.

She was dependent.

I was not.

We were inches apart. His skin still warm from mine. His breath steady. He had to look directly at me when he said it.

"I'll divorce her."

I believed him.

That is the part that stings in retrospect. I believed him not because I was foolish, but because everything else in him felt decisive. When he chose a restaurant, it was the best. When he chose a road, it was the scenic one. When he bought a bike, it was the right one.

Of course he would divorce her.

That was the first lie.

The thing about undercover men is that they learn to compartmentalize. They build boxes in their minds. Label them. Close them. Stack them neatly.

Wife.

Girlfriend.

Daughter.

Court.

Sex.

Future.

Each in its own sealed container.

But boxes crack.

And that night, I heard the faintest sound of something splitting at the seam.

I ignored it.

I was still building brick and chandeliers and heated floors. I was still winning.

I thought the shaky bridge was something I was constructing for him.

I did not yet understand that he had built one for me.

The Birth of Sugar

Somewhere between hauling drywall and seducing a criminal attorney, I became Sugar.

It started with beads.

Vintage Japanese glass beads dusted in crystalline sparkle like they'd been rolled in sugar. They came in colors as bright as cereal, little bumpy spheres that caught thc light and held it. They were expensive. I bought them by the thousands.

To keep that vendor happy, I told her I was naming my company after them.

Sugar Beads & Company.

It stuck.

My name, Gay, had always confused people. Introductions were awkward. My children would groan when I said it out loud to their friends.

But Sugar?

People smiled.

"Hi, Sugar."

It was impossible to say without softening.

Eventually, Sugar Beads & Company became The Sugar Factory. The building demanded something larger. Gay Isber's Design Lab. Later, simply Sugar.

There was only one Sugar Gay Isber.

And now there was a factory.

The Crystal Heist

The chandeliers were the madness.

I couldn't find what I wanted in Canada, so I hunted eBay like a bloodhound. Maria Theresa chandeliers. Glass arms. Cascades of crystal. Baubles like frozen rain.

I bought them all.

Thousands of eBay purchases behind me, I was fearless. I shipped them to Niagara. Drove down every few weeks to collect my treasures.

Then the freight company called.

"You need to come tomorrow. They're outside."

Outside?

When I arrived, there were pallets in the parking lot. Wrapped in plastic. Taller than my Saturn.

My swimming friend had insisted on coming along. Thank God for her.

We stared at the mountain of boxes.

Then we began.

Three hours of surgical unpacking. Every screw was kept with its chandelier. Every crystal was protected. Packaging stripped away. Spatial Tetris at a professional level.

When we were done, the Saturn Vue had become a mobile crystal cave.

Chandeliers in her lap. Crystal at her feet. Arms and prisms stacked to the ceiling. Not an inch of air left unused.

At the border, the guard peered in.

"Anything to declare?"

I laughed.

"Yes."

I paid the duty. Worth every penny.

Back at the building, one of my soup kitchen hires turned out to be a chandelier savant. He could look at a pile of crystal and instinctively know its order. Within days, they were assembled.

If I had bought one of those chandeliers locally, it would have cost what I paid for the entire carload.

Instead, every room would glow.

The Yellow Rose

From the day I bought the building, I knew that corner mattered.

It sat at a four-way stop. Traffic paused there. Engines idled. Drivers waited. It was a stage, whether anyone acknowledged it or not.

The new double glass doors were beautiful, but thcy were set slightly down the façade. The signage was elegant, but it did not command attention.

I wanted something that would stop traffic without shouting.

Something that would feel inevitable.

The Yellow Rose of Texas had lived in my heart long before the building did. A nod to where I came from. A nod to my late husband. A nod to the psychic who once told me he was still watching, still nudging.

The seed money that had purchased my first house in Canada came from him. The sale of that house funded this building.

The rose was not a decoration.

It was lineage.

I bought rolls of non-tarnishing roofing metal. Silver, pliable, luminous. It looked like jewelry before I even touched it.

I sat outside on the concrete and began cutting each petal by hand.

Leaf by leaf. Curve by curve.

I hammered texture into the metal to define the veins, to give the petals dimension. Repoussé in spirit if not in name. The building would wear its own brooch.

My workers held the pieces in place while I directed the screws into the brick. Stainless steel. Secure. Five courses up the corner, climbing two stories tall.

By late afternoon, traffic thickened. More cars idled at the stop.

I didn't know whether to feel exposed or triumphant.

To me, it was already perfect.

It was exactly what I had drawn in my mind the day I first stared at that corner through the windshield while a train blocked my way.

Then windows rolled down.

"It looks great!"

High fives. Thumbs up. Strangers leaning out to affirm something I had already known but had never needed confirmed.

The rose climbed the brick like it had always belonged there.

It was Texas in Ontario.

It was grief turned into steel.

It was gratitude hammered into shape.

And in that moment, standing beneath a two-story blossom I had carved myself, I felt something settle inside me.

This building was not a gamble.

It was an inheritance transformed.

The Yellow Rose of Texas marked it as mine.

And for years after I moved on, it still clung to that brick.

I hope it's still there.

Building the Legend

I named the space The Sugar Factory – Gay Isber's Design Lab before it was finished.

I bossed men around with a smile. Fed them breakfast. Paid them in cash. Drove them home in time for dinner. They worked harder for kindness than they ever had for authority.

Inspectors were greeted warmly. Neighbors given tours. Curiosity turned into anticipation.

I worked with a local glass manufacturer to template every arched window. Each pane was traced by hand. Double-glazed replacements installed. The building tightened its breath and became airtight for the first time in a century.

Downstairs: white marble mosaic, like sugar sparkling cubes, covered my office walls all the way up to the 12-foot ceiling. A black-and-white floor. I created a seven-foot chandelier by stacking three chandeliers and it was framed by twelve-foot arched windows. Modern fixtures from the 60s that I found at thrift stores changed the cadence. It looked like Architectural Digest had decided to relocate to Ontario.

Upstairs: three massive chandeliers in procession over a long, frosted glass table, creating a wall of sparkle. Stainless industrial appliances and giant sink. Heated bathroom floors. Granite slabs rescued from a monument yard were artistically laid. A livestock watering trough, a nod to my Texas roots, was the bathtub. Wide shelving planks turned into custom floors, stained by my own hands until the color was perfect.

I got high on polyurethane and ambition.

The place shimmered. And I was delighted.

The Opening

For the grand opening, I served Texas chili.

A local creamery made chocolate ice cream infused with a whisper of chili heat. Texas Chocolate. Local beer. Laughter everywhere.

I wore a jacket that said, Hi, I'm Gay.

The joke never got old.

The media came. The Globe and Mail. Design features. Photographs of chandeliers raining light over jewelry displays and art and brick.

It became known as one of the first live-work industrial rehabs in the region.

When you climbed the metal stairs to the second story where I lived, you saw nothing until you reached the top.

Then it revealed itself.

The room inhaled you.

I never tired of that reveal.

The Blink

That night, after the last guest left, after the laughter quieted and the chandeliers hummed softly, Seamus crawled into my bed upstairs in the palace I had built from dust.

He looked around like a man standing inside a miracle.

"You did this," he said.

Yes.

I did.

I turned toward him in the glow of the crystals.

"So," I asked lightly, "how's the divorce coming?"

He blinked.

Once.

Twice.

I watched it happen.

The calculation.

The compartment opening.

The box closing again.

He could not say the words.

All that brick. All that crystal. All that proof of my power.

And he could not say there was a divorce underway.

In his eyes, I saw something shift.

In mine, something hardened.

It was the best day of my life.

And the beginning of the end.

The High Tide

After the grand opening, the world widened.

Television segments. Newspaper spreads. Design features. The Sugar Factory became shorthand for audacity.

Then the real leap came.

A national wholesale company approached me to design an entire collection. My work would be sold across Canada. Retailers from coast to coast.

Sugar was no longer a building.

It was a brand.

Dark Sugar. Edgier, heavier chains. A whisper of leather and rebellion.

Powdered Sugar. White-on-white. Soft shimmer. Bridal light.

Sugar Sprinkles. Playful. Youthful. Candy colors.

Eight collections in total, each one carrying the story forward.

At the launch convention, a local candy manufacturer flooded the room with mountains of sweets. I made the owner a crown from crystal beads shaped like her candy. She wore it back to her family company as proof that Sugar had blessed them.

It was theatrical. It was joyful.

Seamus stood there watching people admire me.

Watching buyers place orders.

Watching cameras turn toward me.

I thought, This is the final shaky bridge. He sees it now. He sees I am not a hobby. I am a force.

I thought I was golden.

I wasn't.

By then, I understood something about placement. About timing. About standing where the turn happens.

The Woman Who Made the Queen Laugh

Borders do not end storms. They relocate them.

I did not plan to meet the Queen of England.

I planned to give her flowers.

The sun was sharp that morning, the kind that makes every color look lacquered and deliberate. The red carpet glowed. The rose garden behind Government House was in full bloom, all ceremony and symmetry. Security moved like a quiet tide along the barricades. Across from me stood the monarchists, flags folded under their arms, faces set in devotion. They had come to be seen.

I had come to give.

In my hands was a bouquet so bright it almost hummed, and a silver tin wrapped in tissue the color of crushed peonies. Inside the tin was a bracelet I had made myself. Pearls the same age as her coronation. Crystal. Silver. Nothing she needed. Nothing she could not buy a thousand times over.

But it was mine.

She was nearing the end of her walkabout. The aides had already begun to angle her toward the waiting car that would take her to the airport, then New York, then whatever came next in a life that had never belonged only to her. She was efficient, elegant, practiced. Smiling, nodding, gloved hands extending and retracting in perfect rhythm.

I felt the moment thinning.

"Your Majesty," I said.

Not loudly. Not desperately. Just clearly.

She turned.

There is something about being looked at by someone whose face has lived on currency your entire life. The blue of her eyes was not pale, as I expected. It was concentrated. Direct. When they met mine, I had the strangest instinct not to blink, as if blinking would close the door.

"I have something for you."

She stepped toward me. Not toward the flags. Not toward the cameras. Toward me.

I handed her the flowers first. She passed them smoothly to her assistant. Then I placed the tin in her gloved hands.

"I made this for you once before," I said, steady now, though my pulse had started to drum. "I gave it to Charles and Camilla when they were here, hoping they might pass it along."

She looked at me.

There was the smallest pause. A flicker. And then she laughed.

It was not a royal laugh. It was not polite. It was amused, almost conspiratorial, as if we both understood something that did not require explanation.

In that split second, I imagined her thinking, Camilla did not give me a thing.

She looked back at me, still smiling, and said something gracious and official, as queens do. But the laugh had already sealed it. I had not been dismissed. I had been seen.

Then she was gone. Into the car. Into history.

And the cameras turned to me.

The thing about royalty is that everyone thinks the magic happens in the center.

It doesn't.

It happens at the turn.

Earlier that day, someone at Government House had taken me aside. Not formally. Not ceremoniously. Just quietly, the way Canadians do everything.

"If you want to see her properly," they said, pointing to a curved stretch of gravel near the end of the garden path, "stand there."

I knew these people. I had made jewelry for the government gift shop. I had delivered tin boxes wrapped in tissue and hope. I had laughed with them. I had shown up. When you are kind to the staff, they remember. When you make their days brighter, they move you a few feet closer to history.

So I stood where they told me.

Not in the center of the crowd. Not elbowing for attention. Not waving a flag.

At the final bend.

By the time she reached me, she had already absorbed the bows and the camera flashes and the careful offerings. The walkabout had done its work. The public had been satisfied. The choreography was complete.

And then there was me.

A woman with a bouquet that refused to be subtle.

A bracelet she did not need.

And the audacity to speak.

It was the placement that changed everything. If I had been in the thick of the scrum, I would have been one more face. One more outstretched hand. But at the end of the line, there was space. A breath. A second that belonged to no one else.

That is where the laugh happened.

That is where I learned something I would spend the rest of my life refining: you do not have to be at the center to be powerful. You have to understand timing. You have to understand turns.

The woman who made the Queen laugh was not born in a palace.

She was born in a hurricane.

The Bargain

Still no Divorce.

Not even after I proved myself more Canadian than him. Not even after the Queen laughed and cameras flashed and I stood in rooms his wife would never enter.

If I mentioned it, something in him cooled.

The word divorce would pass between us like smoke and then vanish. The air shifted. His jaw tightened almost imperceptibly. The file drawer closed.

So I stopped asking directly.

I started negotiating.

I told myself I was adventurous. Confident. Evolved.

But I was bargaining.

Seamus didn't need to demand anything. He would describe. That was enough. He had a way of speaking about desire as if it were theoretical. Hypothetical. Something other couples did. Something curious people explored.

He never pushed.

He planted.

He would lean back and say, "I've always wondered what that would be like."

And I would hear it as a challenge.

He wanted a threesome.

I arranged it.

Not because I wanted her.

Because I wanted him.

Because I thought if I could be the woman who did what his wife wouldn't, I would become indispensable. I would become the upgrade.

I can still smell her perfume. It clung to the sheets long after she left. I told myself I liked it. I told myself I was modern, fearless, unthreatened.

The truth?

I was performing fearlessness.

He wanted novelty.

I became novelty.

Arizona. Red rock and heat. Rented bikes slicing through desert highways. Anonymous sex clubs where no one knew our names and everything pulsed with possibility. We walked into rooms where curiosity was currency. We kissed in corners like we were starring in our own rebellion.

It felt intoxicating.

It also felt like a test.

If I am doing this for you, what are you doing for me?

I never said it exactly like that.

But it was in every glance.

When do I get you without the wife hovering like a legal footnote?

When do I stop competing with someone I've never met?

Why have I never seen your children?

That question always made him smooth.

He would tilt his head. Smile. Courtroom calm. Redirect.

"We're not there yet."

"Timing is complicated."

"You know how custody works."

Then he would offer something shiny.

A hockey game in Toronto.
A weekend near Honey Harbor.
A last-minute flight.
A promise of space, someday.

He dangled experience.

He never dangled resolution.

And I kept escalating.

Because the more unstable it felt, the more I tried to stabilize it with intensity.

More sex.
More access.
More proof that I was different.

I was slowly disappearing into the performance of being chosen.

The wife existed like a shadow I wasn't allowed to name. The divorce lived in the air but never on paper. If I pressed too hard, he withdrew. If I played along, he glowed.

He kept me juiced on possibility.

Just enough intimacy to keep me hopeful.
Just enough mystery to keep me off balance.

That is the part no one tells you about manipulation.

It doesn't feel like control.

It feels like you're almost winning.

Until you realize you've been competing in a game that was never designed to end.

The Lake

Twice we rented the lake cabin.

I mailed clothes ahead so the saddlebags on his bike would stay empty for food and wine. Efficiency disguised as romance. I curated the illusion of spontaneity. I handled logistics so he could feel untethered.

We rented a small aluminum boat and motored to a tiny island in the middle of a crystalline Ontario lake. Granite, pine, wild blueberries, silence. No neighbors. No witnesses.

We stripped before the engine ticked cool.

There is something about lying naked on sun-warmed rock that makes you believe you are outside consequence. We swam in water so clear it erased edges. Ate bread and cheese. Smoked cigars. Read the New York Times like civilized exiles. Scotch in the afternoon. Red wine at dusk.

It looked like freedom.

It was theater.

The moment we were fully exposed, the boats appeared.

They always did.

Small fishing boats with one or two men. They drifted close enough to see but far enough to deny. Lines cast lazily into the water. Motors idling. Eyes sliding sideways.

Hovering.

Not fishing.

Watching.

I laughed the first time.

"Coincidence."

Seamus did not laugh.

He leaned back on his elbows and watched them watch me.

There was something electric in him. Not protectiveness. Not jealousy.

Display.

As if my body were proof of his dominance. As if exposure were part of the ritual.

And I knew - in a place I did not want to examine - that if he could have invited them onto the rock and staged something obscene while he remained fully in control, he might have.

Not because he wanted to share me.

Because he wanted to orchestrate appetite.

And I was still trying to win.

That is the feral part no one admits.

You think you are liberated. You think you are daring. You think you are rewriting the rules.

But you are responding.

At night, the island changed.

The lake went black and breathless. The stars pressed low. I would serve him dinner on that rock like a queen in exile. Steak done precisely how he liked it. Potatoes heavy with butter. Something indulgent. Something that said, I see you. I feed you. I am essential.

That was when the raccoons came.

A whole family. Thick, fearless, deliberate.

Seamus did not hesitate.

He tore off bread and crouched.

They approached him without flinching.

One by one, those wild animals placed their small hands against his fingers and took food from his palm. Their eyes never left him. They trusted the offering.

He fed them slowly.

Not enough to satisfy.

Just enough to keep them close.

And I watched.

I watched those fat raccoons override instinct for hunger. I watched them recalibrate fear into dependency.

And something in me registered the symmetry.

He understood conditioning.

Reward.

Withhold.

Reward again.

Just enough affection to keep me leaning forward.

Just enough mystery to keep me destabilized.

Just enough pleasure to keep me convinced I was choosing this.

There was still no divorce.

No paperwork.

No separation.

Only postponement stretched thin as fishing line.

The lake was clean and cold.

I was not.

I was being trained to mistake intensity for intimacy.

And by then, I was already hooked.

The lake was clear.

The future was not.

The Real Competition

I stopped asking about love.

I started asking about leverage.

Journalist without the notebook. Voice soft. Questions casual. I let him talk.

Eventually, he revealed what actually mattered.

Her family had money.

Not lottery money.
Not startup money.
Television evangelist money.
Early broadcast empire money.
Generational money that builds institutions and names buildings after itself.

She had the certificate.

She had the children.

She had absorbed his scandal years before - the child he fathered with another woman - and folded it into the marriage like it was an inconvenient receipt.

She did not erupt.

She consolidated.

While I was dangling ecstasy, she was anchoring legacy.

That was the moment something inside me went cold.

I was negotiating with desire.

She was negotiating with permanence.

Sex is currency.

But security is infrastructure.

And Seamus understood infrastructure.

He could disappear for hours and reappear composed.
He could speak in hypotheticals while protecting assets.
He could confess just enough to look transparent while revealing nothing that cost him.

My world was heat.

Hers was contracts.

I had built a palace of sensation.

I had built a brand.
A summer.
A mythology.

And he had not moved a single legal piece on the board.

Not one filing.
Not one public shift.
Not one risk.

That was when I understood the hierarchy.

I was the adrenaline.

She was the foundation.

Adrenaline is thrilling.

Foundations endure.

And men who live double lives do not gamble their foundations unless the reward exceeds the risk.

I had been trying to outshine structure with passion.

That is not how power works.

So I stopped trying to be better.

I started trying to be irreplaceable.

That was the pivot.

That was when obsession stopped being romantic and started being strategic.

I was not competing with a woman. I was competing with a system.

British Columbia

We flew west for the grand motorcycle loop.

Harley rented. Washington State carved into the itinerary. Six days of mountain air and turquoise lakes.

He sneezed the entire flight because a dog sat in the row ahead of us. Allergic, irritated, still charming.

I had burned a CD filled with every version of Somewhere Over the Rainbow I could find. Jazz versions. Hawaiian versions. Indie covers. Orchestral sweeps. I sang it loud and proud over the roar of the Harley.

On the back of the bike, jacket open, bra off, and breasts bared, the wind against my skin, I sang them all.

It felt cinematic. Trees lining the highway like cathedral columns. Beetle-killed forests fading into impossible blue water.

Cabins. Wine. Laughter.

It looked like perfection.

Until the phone rang.

The Balcony

It was a roadside hotel. Beige carpet. Ice machine humming down the hall. Nothing romantic. Just transit.

The phone rang.

His wife.

He was standing there in nothing but his briefs when he answered. For half a second he looked startled, like he'd forgotten which life he was in.

Then instinct took over.

He moved fast.

Out the sliding door. Onto the balcony. Bare feet on cold concrete. Overlooking a parking lot full of pickup trucks and pine trees.

Like he was still in Toronto.
Like geography could erase context.

I stayed inside.

I didn't move.

I listened.

I did not exist in that conversation.

There was no mention of where he was.
No mention of who he was with.

No acknowledgment of the body still warm in the room behind him.

His voice changed.

Softer. Familiar. Domestic.

I heard him say he would see her Wednesday.

I heard him say he loved her.

Not forced. Not careful. Fluent.

I cracked the door just enough to be certain I wasn't inventing it.

I wasn't.

The rage was not loud.

It was volcanic and silent.

I wanted to tip his motorcycle onto its side.
Drag it across the asphalt.
Shred every shirt he owned.
Walk to the highway and flag down the first logging truck headed anywhere but here.

But there was no car.

No exit.

We were surrounded by forest and two-lane road and nowhere.

And in that stillness, something colder than rage settled in.

Clarity.

If he could speak to her like that while naked from the waist down and seconds removed from me, then he could speak to me like that too.

Love was modular.

He was a master of compartments.

Boxes stacked neatly inside him.

In one box, he was my lover on a sun-warmed island.
In another, he was husband and father.
In another, courtroom authority.

He could stand exposed in one world and conduct business in another without a flicker.

That was not confusion.

That was skill.

That night there was no sleep for me.

He came back inside. Slid under the covers. Snored within minutes.

I lay awake staring at the ceiling, counting the spaces between his breaths.

Listening to the sound of a man who could divide himself without bleeding.

And I understood something I would never unlearn.

I was not the only room in his house.

I was just the one with the lights on.

The Realization

I had done everything.

Lavish trips.
Equal footing on expenses.
Adventure.
Affection.
Devotion.
Escalation.

I had built a palace.

Built a brand.
Built a summer so curated it felt mythic.

Why wouldn't he choose me?

That was the ego talking.

Why wouldn't he?

I had rolled out the red carpet so many times it no longer felt like effort. It felt like proof.

Proof that I was superior.
Proof that I was braver.
Proof that I could out-love anyone.

But on that balcony, listening to him say I love you into the dark, something cracked.

He wasn't choosing between better and worse.

He was choosing between structure and sensation.

And structure almost always wins.

Structure holds bank accounts.
Structure holds children.
Structure holds last names and inheritances and church pews and courtrooms.

Sensation holds heat.

Heat fades.

That was the cut.

Not that he loved her more.

Not that he desired me less.

But that I had mistaken intensity for leverage.

He did not need to choose.

He could compartmentalize and keep both.

That was the real revelation.

I was not competing.

I was supplementing.

The next morning, I was quiet.

The ride continued.

Miles unspooled under the tires. Pine and asphalt and wind. His hand occasionally brushing my thigh like nothing had shifted.

But everything had.

I did not confront him.

I did not end it.

I did not snap my fingers and say next, even though a stronger woman might have.

Instead, I went still.

And stillness, for me, is never surrender.

It is calculation.

If he could live in boxes, so could I.

If he could run parallel lives, I could learn the blueprint.

This was the moment obsession changed shape.

It stopped being hunger.

It became study.

I stopped asking to be chosen.

I started asking why he needed compartments at all.

That was the awakening.

Not loud.

Not dramatic.

Cold.

And once you see the architecture of a man, you can never go back to believing the performance.

I made a plan.

A fast one.

And for the first time, it wasn't about winning him.

It was about understanding the game.

That was the day I stopped being feral and started being observant.

The Screenplay

On the plane home, I pivoted.

If sex could not secure him,
if brick and crystal could not secure him,
then I would secure his legend.

"Let's write a movie," I said.

His head turned slowly.

Not amused. Not dismissive.

Alert.

"A movie about your undercover years. But set in thc U.S. Bigger market. Bigger money. Motorcycle gangs. A chapter president dying. The power struggle to replace him. Loyalty. Betrayal. Informants inside the inner circle."

I watched it land.

His spine straightened.

I had finally found the vein.

He had always told the stories in fragments. Over scotch. On long drives. In bed. They were currency to him. Proof of danger. Proof of brilliance. Proof he had lived in rooms most men never enter.

Now I was offering permanence.

"You'll be the technical consultant," I said. "On set. Making sure it's real. Your name attached. Your world translated."

That was the key.

Not love.

Legacy.

Zap.

The temperature shifted.

I was no longer the sulking girlfriend in the hotel room.

I was the architect of his myth.

I took my laptop everywhere.

Poolside at nudist resorts. On balconies overlooking water. In rented cabins. Between courthouse visits. We wrote beside naked strangers in Florida sun while champagne glasses sweated on plastic tables.

It looked decadent.

It was transactional.

He paid me.

It was cheaper than a ghostwriter.

And I was good.

We nearly got it optioned. A director with Easy Rider connections. Meetings. Phone calls. Momentum building just enough to keep us leaning forward.

The story was combustible.

A motorcycle club president dying.
Who would take the throne.
South Dakota rally grounds thick with engines and testosterone.
Alliances shifting.
Undercover threads woven tight enough to choke.

We even traveled to the rally so I could feel it. Smell the asphalt. Hear the engines rattle through bone.

Another excuse to stay near him.

Another tether.

Another reason for the phone to ring and for me to be necessary.

But underneath the productivity, something else was happening.

I was no longer writing a screenplay.

I was buying proximity.

If I could not be wife, I would be indispensable collaborator.

If I could not have structure, I would build narrative.

I told myself this was power.

But it was still orbit.

The difference was this:

Now I understood the gravity.

And I was choosing to stay in it.

That was the darkest part.

It was slowly killing me.

Not because he was cruel.

Because I had finally seen the system and decided to keep playing anyway.

Sympathy with the Devil

He loved telling stories about Sturgis.

Undercover work.
Motorcycle gangs.
Drug deals where sampling was expected but he somehow wriggled out clean.
The inside skinny on massive Canadian busts.
The long con.
The patience.
The hero narrative.

He lit up when he talked about it.

He loved the bad boys.
He loved infiltrating them.
He loved belonging without belonging.

I already knew his stories by heart. I had catalogued them. Filed them away like scenes.

So I would lean in and say,
"What about that one in Montreal?"
"What about Sturgis?"
"What about the bust where the guy pulled the gun?"

His eyes would brighten. Hook set.

We started calling it *Sympathy with the Devil.*

I made him the main character.
I slipped in the details that made him human.

He hated hamburgers.
Everyone always tried to hand him a hamburger.
He'd peel back the bun like it was an insult.

Tacos weren't his thing either.
He was a war hero in biker bars but picky about condiments.

Those contradictions made him dimensional. I knew that. I knew story.

And he loved that I knew story.

I learned quickly that "Let's work on the screenplay" was my golden key.

"Come over. I'll cook. We'll drink scotch. We'll write."

He would be there.

Then it became travel.

"There's a nudist resort in Florida. Three days. Bring your laptop."

"Let's take the bike to Ottawa. I've got a case. We'll write at night."

"Montreal. Great hotel. Client's paying. We'll write."

Rinse. Repeat.

Every trip was framed as creative collaboration.

Every weekend was billed as legacy building.

He believed in this project because I made him the hero of it.

And because hiring me was still cheaper than hiring a real ghostwriter.

I told myself I was securing his legacy.

What I was really securing was proximity.

When the writing phase ended, I shifted gears.

Registration.
Copyright.
Editing passes.
Query letters.
Producer lists.
Follow-ups.

The unsexy work.

Not the naked Florida afternoons.
Not the motorcycle rides through Quebec.
Not the scotch at midnight while he described gang hierarchies.

The grind.

And then it started happening.

Emails back.

"Let's talk."

"Interesting material."

"Who represents this?"

We were no longer fantasizing.
We were in motion.

And then came the one that mattered.

The big name.

The call.

Hollywood Calls

The night the producer call was scheduled, we stayed at a newly opened hotel in downtown Toronto.

Polished. Glassy. Designed to impress people who needed to feel important.

I paid for it.

We ordered tempura crab so delicate it shattered under the slightest pressure, served in a wine glass like edible jewels. Champagne in bed. The sheets crisp and white and untouched by history.

Exhaustion. Anticipation. Victory hovering just above us.

We took the call naked.

Glowing.

We sounded like partners.

We sounded inevitable.

The next morning I drove back to the Sugar Factory, still buoyed by momentum. The skyline shrinking in the rearview mirror. I replayed phrases from the call. Meetings. Next steps. Possibility.

Then my phone rang.

It was him.

I answered.

Silence.

Then I heard it.

His car.

Road noise.

And her voice.

He had butt-dialed me.

I did not breathe.

She was talking about a condo downtown. Near the hockey rink. Walking distance to games. Investment strategy. Practical. Thoughtful. Permanent.

He responded easily.

Comfortably.

There was no tension in his voice.

No hesitation.

No fracture.

He had never mentioned a condo.

Not once.

I hung up.

My hands were shaking.

The phone rang again.

Him.

Another butt-dial.

This time I let it run longer.

Laughter.

Domestic logistics.

Her tone warm and proprietary.

The kind of conversation that assumes decades.

I hung up again.

The phone rang a third time.

Three accidental windows into a life I was not in.

I heard negotiation.

I heard partnership.

I heard love.

The movie was ours.

The condo was hers.

And suddenly the math was clean.

He was building two futures at once.

One fueled by adrenaline and myth and creative electricity.

The other anchored in equity and brick and shared calendars.

And I was financing one of them.

The hotel.

The travel.

The writing.

The illusion of collaboration.

I pulled the car to the side of the road because the blood drained from my body so fast I thought I might faint.

This was not confusion.

This was architecture.

He was not torn.

He was diversified.

And for the first time, I understood the scale of it.

I had not been competing.

I had been underwriting.

The Countermove

The next day when he called, I smiled into the phone.

"My birthday is coming up," I said. "Let's do something different."

He didn't hesitate.

He offered his best friend.

A beach. A fire. A picnic. Three bikes cutting down the highway like a procession.

I accepted.

Not because I wanted the friend.

Because I wanted access.

Access to someone who had known him longer. Someone who might loosen a thread. Someone who might reveal what Seamus kept contained.

What I did not anticipate was this:

Seamus had designed the evening.

Not for pleasure.

For observation.

He wanted to watch.

To curate.

To control the tempo.

To test something.

And what Seamus did not anticipate was this:

His friend was not an accessory.

He was present.

Grounded.

Attentive in a way that startled me.

There was no performance in him. No need to dominate the room. No appetite masquerading as intimacy.

The touch was different.

Not hungry.

Not claiming.

Curious.

Responsive.

And in that contrast, something inside me split open.

I had told myself I was addicted to the chemistry with Seamus.

I wasn't.

I was addicted to orbiting power.

Seamus was appetite.

His friend was connection.

And that night, on that stretch of sand with the fire burning low and the bikes cooling behind us, I felt something I had not felt in months.

Centered.

Not showcased.

Not consumed.

Centered.

The revelation was almost embarrassing.

I had been compensating.

Overperforming.

Escalating.

Not because Seamus was extraordinary in bed.

But because he was extraordinary at controlling the frame.

He was magnetic in story, in authority, in secrecy.

In intimacy, he was self-focused.

His friend did not need to orchestrate.

He was simply there.

And that is when the addiction clarified itself.

It was never about sex.

It was about proximity to dominance.

Seamus had trained me to equate volatility with intensity.

His friend offered something steadier.

And for a split second - a dangerous, quiet second - I understood that I could walk away.

Not because I was outraged.

But because the spell cracked.

Seamus saw it too.

I watched the flicker in his face.

The recalibration.

He had opened a door to test me.

Instead, he exposed himself.

I also learned things that night about Seamus that he never meant for me to know.

Not secrets spoken aloud.

Secrets revealed by contrast.

That was the real counter move.

Not jealousy.

Awakening.

I had mistaken electricity for intimacy.

The Storm

On the drive back from that wicked little weekend, we stopped for coffee and gas.

When his friend went inside, it was just Seamus and me.

I said it plainly.

"I want you to get a divorce. Or I want this to be over."

He didn't flinch.

"Well," he said, almost casually, "the commute to the Sugar Factory is getting hard anyway. Maybe it's good if we cool it."

That was it.

No explosion.
No argument.
Just a quiet deflection lobbed back into my chest.

I think I stopped breathing.

I had pushed.
He had responded.
Not with passion.
Not with fight.

With withdrawal.

He dropped me at the Sugar Factory. The two of them rode back toward Toronto, engines fading.

I stood there for a second before unlocking the door.

I still believed the worst thing that had happened that day was the conversation in the parking lot.

I was wrong.

Water

The smell hit first.

Then the silence.

Then the sound of water still dripping somewhere it shouldn't.

A microburst had torn through while we were gone.

The flat roof's old central drain had shifted at the roofline. Instead of channeling rain down and away, it had poured it straight into the building.

Two stories of water.

Inches of it.

The floors I had stained by hand buckled in waves. The wide boards warped and lifted like ribs. The black and white tile curled at the corners. Mold was already breathing along the edges of the walls.

Jewelry rusting.
Fabrics soaked.
Chairs swollen.
Water seeping from drawers.

It looked like a slow-motion tsunami had passed through and settled into stillness.

Everything I had built with intention and force was now soft and ruined.

He had just cooled us.

The building had drowned.

The metaphor was not subtle.

Collapse

I stood there in the middle of the second floor and felt something in me cave inward.

It wasn't dramatic.

It was hollow.

Call insurance.
Call workers.
Photograph everything.
Drag what could be saved outside.
Start again.

He was on his motorcycle somewhere between cities.
Even if I had called, he wouldn't have answered.

And even if he had answered, what would he have done?

Water, water everywhere.

The Sugar Factory, my crystal palace, the symbol of everything I had proven to the world and to him, reduced to soggy wood and the smell of rot.

It was the lowest I had been in years.

I had tried ego.
Sex.
Art.
Myth.
Money.

Legend.
Leverage.

And now nature had entered the conversation.

There is something almost biblical about that moment.

When you build too fast.
When you love too hard.
When you refuse to see the signs.

Sometimes the sky answers.

Phoenix Logic

I grabbed what I could.

Insurance covered the hotel. The building would be closed for a month. Heaters roared. Industrial fans screamed. Boards were ripped up. The floors I had stained with my own hands were torn out like muscle from bone.

The smell of rot felt personal.

Friends came.
Workers returned.
Insurance adjusters calculated.
I cried quietly and then stopped crying because there was work to do.

Income froze. Jewelry parties paused. Orders stalled. Cash flow shrank.

It was not jump-off-a-bridge despair.

It was colder than that.

It was:
You are starting again.
Now what?

The building would never feel the same.

Something in it had shifted.
Something in me had shifted.

Lying in that hotel bed paid for by insurance, I began rearranging the chessboard.

Repair it.
Let insurance pay.
Make it beautiful again.
Then move.

Move closer to him.

If distance was the excuse, remove the distance.

I didn't tell anyone.

When I eventually mentioned selling, it was like announcing a death in the community. That building had become more than brick. It was spectacle. It was belonging. It was chandeliers and wine and neighborhood pride.

But pride does not hold a man.

And I was still addicted.

We danced around each other for weeks.
"If you don't get a divorce, don't call me."
He called.
I answered.

It felt like oxygen.

He visited the building while repairs were underway. He comforted me. Cuddled me. Played supportive. But I did not reveal my plan.

Not yet.

You never reveal the bomb before it's armed.

Reopening

The building reopened softly.

New boards.
Repolished surfaces.
Repaired ceilings.
A brave little relaunch.

Thank God for insurance. I barely remembered signing the policy. It saved me from ruin.

But the joy was muted.

It was like rebuilding after a fire. Beautiful, yes. But smoke still lived in the memory.

I called a real estate agent.

"Come over. Let's talk."

And quietly, I listed it.

Then I searched.

Bay and Bloor.

Yorkville.

I found it.

A two-story penthouse in the sky.

Glass walls. Views to the lake. Views toward the U.S. On another wall, the University of Toronto. The Royal Ontario Museum. The pulse of the city beneath you.

Private elevator.
Curved glass ceilings.
Wood-burning fireplace.
Mirrors everywhere, infinite reflections.
A marble bathroom that looked sculpted rather than installed.
Sauna.
Chef's kitchen.
Penny tile.
Marble floors.
Catwalk above.

It looked like the final residence of someone extravagant and unrepentant. ZaZa?

It was spectacular.

And it was rentable.

By selling the Sugar Factory, I could afford it.

More importantly, it placed me in his world.

No more commute excuse.

No more distance.

I called him.

"Meet me."

We rode the elevator up. The doors opened into sky.

He walked to the glass and looked down over Toronto. Over the water. Over the skyline.

"This," I said, "is going to be my new place."

The phoenix version of me.

Not small town artisan.

Not crystal palace in exile.

Yorkville penthouse.

In his backyard.

The Toronto Police Service just down the street.

I was coming to him.

He couldn't say no.

Or so I believed.

Yorkville on Credit

He stood in the penthouse, staring out over Toronto.

His city.
His streets.
His police force.
His restaurants.
His secrets.

Floor-to-ceiling glass. The skyline laid out like a territory map.

I watched the shock move through him.

I had not warned him.

No hints.
No softening.
No slow reveal.

I had simply signed.

Made decisions I would never advise anyone else to make.

Had my son adjust documents.
Proved income that was aspirational at best.
Spoke numbers out loud as if conviction alone could solidify them.

It almost didn't matter.

I had been burning money for this man for years.

Flights. Hotels. Weekends. Production meetings. Gasoline and champagne and curated experiences.

What was one more blaze?

This one had scale.

Glass ceilings.
Mirrored walls.
Marble bath.
Sauna.
A catwalk in the sky that made you feel suspended above consequence.

Yorkville.

On credit.

He walked from window to window like a king surveying a conquered province.

I could feel it - the shift.

This was not sensation.

This was status.

And for a moment, I had matched him.

Matched the scale of his double life.

Matched the audacity.

Matched the architecture.

But beneath the gleam, the numbers were rotting.

Credit cards stretched thin enough to hum.

The building sale delayed.

Closing pushed from Friday to Monday.

"Technicality," the realtor said.

"It'll go through."

It had to.

Because I was operating on fumes.

Because the down payment was bravado layered over debt.

Because if the sale collapsed, so did the illusion.

He did not know that.

He saw the view.

He saw the marble.

He saw the woman who could secure a penthouse without blinking.

He did not see the quiet panic calculating interest rates in the background.

I was not buying a home.

I was buying position.

If I could not secure him with heat, with myth, with screenplay momentum —

I would secure him with altitude.

I thought if I raised the stakes high enough, he would have to choose.

But that is the thing about men who live in compartments.

They do not merge worlds just because you upgrade the view.

They simply enjoy both.

And that night, standing above the city on borrowed money, I understood something brutal:

I was not outplaying him.

I was outspending myself.

I thought elevation would equal commitment. It only increased the fall.

The Last Night

The night before leaving the Sugar Factory, my son stood beside me in the dark.

He had come to help me relocate.

He did not ask many questions.

We burned photographs.

Remember when prints came with doubles for a penny?
Stacks of them.
Glossy proof that something had once been solid.

I had years of duplicates.

Smiling faces.
Christmas mornings.
Vacations.
Men who promised permanence.

We fed them into metal bins behind the building.

One after another.

The flames curled the edges first. Then the faces blackened. Then the paper folded inward on itself like it was embarrassed to exist.

Smoke lifted straight into the night.

I did not cry.

I was not sentimental.

I was reducing weight.

I whittled my life down to what could fit into a truck.

Sold furniture cheap.
Gave friends deals they'll never see again.
Watched them carry away pieces of rooms I had once curated like art installations.

Ten dollars felt like oxygen.

Twenty felt like reprieve.

I wasn't downsizing.

I was liquidating.

Every dollar bought time.

I watched my bank balance like a heart monitor in an ICU.

Up a little.
Down a little.
Flatline threatening.

It only needed to hold until Monday.

Just hold.

Because Monday meant closing.

Monday meant the building sale going through.

Monday meant the penthouse wasn't a hallucination.

Monday meant I had not set my life on fire for a view.

Behind me, the metal bins glowed.

Photographs collapsing into ash.

I told myself this was cleansing.

But if I am honest, it was escalation.

You do not burn archives unless you are preparing for impact.

And somewhere in that smoke, I knew:

There was no safe return after this.

I was not starting over. I was doubling down.

Military Precision

The moving truck had to be back by two sharp.

If I was thirty minutes late, my credit card would decline.

There was no backup plan.
No one to call.

We picked up the truck at night.
Loaded in the dark.
Drove before dawn.
Beat traffic if possible.
Pray.

Seven of us.
My ragtag boys.
Loyal.
Kind.
Unaware I was as financially fragile as they were.

We reached Yorkville mid-morning.

Forty-eight stories up waited the penthouse.

But first, the truck.

The only way to beat the clock was to empty everything immediately.

So we did.

The Curb

We unloaded my life onto the sidewalk.

Rosenthal china.
Christofle silver.
Baccarat glass.
Boxes of beads.
Vintage findings from eBay.
Furniture from Texas.
Furniture from Waterloo.
Furniture from Kitchener.

Decades of taste and labor and reinvention stacked on concrete in Yorkville.

It looked like a garage sale for someone who had fallen from orbit.

People slowed.

"How much for this?"

"Is that for sale?"

"Are you moving out?"

Some didn't even wait for answers. Hands reached into boxes. Lifted glass. Turned silver over in their palms. Weighed it.

My life, handled like surplus.

It was humiliating.

Absurd.

Necessary.

The truck deadline loomed. Everything had to be off the rental. Off the meter. Off the books.

My son moved efficiently. No commentary. No softness.

The truck pulled away.

We drove back from the rental lot.

When we returned, strangers were circling my belongings like gulls.

For one sharp second I thought:

This is insane.

What am I doing?

Then Seamus arrived.

He pulled up and saw it all.

My entire world on the curb.

The penthouse above.
The china below.
The illusion suspended between.

He stood there, half-smiling, half-stunned.

He did not step forward and take control.

He did not say, "Let's move this inside."

He did not reach for his wallet.

He did not say, "Are you okay?"

He watched.

Like it was a spectacle.

Like I had staged it.

I wanted somcthing small and human.

I wanted him to cross the street to Subway and bring back a sandwich.

I wanted him to notice I hadn't eaten all day.

I wanted him to ask.

But I could not tell him I was broke.

Broke meant weak.

Broke meant I had miscalculated.

Broke meant I had built altitude without foundation.

So I smiled.

I introduced my son.

"This is Frank."

Frank did not smile.

He did not extend warmth.

He did not pretend.

He had heard the stories.

He knew the cost.

He saw the orbit I had trapped myself in.

His lip tightened almost imperceptibly.

Then he turned his back.

Frank was honest.

He was not going to protect the man who had unraveled his mother.

Seamus stood there, hands in pockets, suspended between involvement and detachment.

Half in.

Half out.

Always half.

And there I was.

Yorkville.

Penthouse in the sky.

Zero dollars liquid.

Life on the curb.

Son fully awake.

Man strategically distant.

That is the real image of that day.

Not the marble bath.
Not the skyline.
Not the catwalk in the clouds.

The curb.

Where I finally understood that I had lifted myself into the air for a man who would not bend down to help me carry a box.

That was the day I stopped trying to impress him and started trying to survive him.

Night One in the Sky

My son left as fast as he could.

Back to Texas.
Back to sanity.
Back to distance.

And I was alone in the penthouse and it was night one.

Forty-eight stories up.
Glass on every wall.
Seamus's city below me.

The windows were filthy.

Not just dusty.
Filthy.

And I decided that was the first thing that had to change.

Why? Exhaustion. Pride. Obsession. All of it.

The upper panels could be lifted out entirely. Heavy double-paned glass, real metal frames. I figured out the mechanics and took them down in pairs. Carried them to the marble bathroom. Stood them in the soaker tub and scrubbed them one by one.

Dried them with my bath towels.

I removed every window before putting a single one back.

That was the miscalculation.

By the time I finished, a serious storm was rolling in. Wind wrapped around that tower like a living thing. Trying to reinstall those panes was like wrestling glass sails on a ship in open water.

Forty-mile-an-hour wind, maybe more.

It was absurd. It was slapstick. It was survival.

So, I gave up. Exhausted and cold.

I piled everything I owned on the bed. Towels. Heaps of clothes. Piles of linens I dumped out of boxes. IKEA bags with blankets and flotsam and jetsam. I crawled underneath the heap and let the wind howl through the open walls of glass.

That was my first night in Yorkville.

No money.
No man.
No windows.

Just grit and a howling wind. I was so thrilled I had cleaned those windows every time I looked at them after that night.

Monday

I woke up energized.

The windows went back in. Sparkling.

I moved like a general under pressure. All of the furniture was placed exactly where I had envisioned it months before so I did not have to move furniture but I did have to hang paintings, place dishes in the cabinets and silverware in the drawers. Everything efficient and deliberate.

I was building theater.

From the catwalk, I suspended a braided sculpture made from white felt rescued from the old Kitchener factory. Felt was originally used under Victrola records at the turn of the century. I cut it into strips, braided it like Rapunzel's hair, threaded in crystals and white lights so it cascaded down in a glowing column.

On one wall, glittered fabric butterflies spiraled upward as I pinned them into place like they were scientific specimens.

Over a round table, I hung a branch I had once begged from a landscaping crew before leaving Kitchener. Painted white. Dusted in blue and glitter. Strung with crystals. Below it, concrete female heads adorned in jewelry like modern muses.

I did it all in one weekend.

I had no money.

I had canned green beans and Diet Coke.

But I was creating.

And creation is oxygen.

The Bank

Monday morning, I walked to the bank.

“Is it in?” I asked.

“It’s in,” she said.

I asked for one hundred dollars.

I was starving.

I walked out lighter than I had in months.

I had survived the curb.
The truck.
The delay.
The gamble.

I was in Yorkville.
Alive. And my account was finally flush.

Now he would see.

The Grandmother

On my way back, the three short blocks, a woman with a suitcase stopped me.

She was lost.

I told her I had just moved in and barely knew my way around myself. She was looking for a car rental agency. Surprisingly, even to myself, I knew it as it was in my building next to Subway. My building had such a delightful ring.

She explained she was in town to see her granddaughter perform that night.

"American Idol," she said.

I hadn't kept up with the show.

Later, I learned it was Jordin Sparks.

But in that moment, she was simply a grandmother in heels, trying to find her way.

I invited her upstairs.

Why not?

My first guest in the penthouse.

She walked through the mirrored halls, ran her hand down the felt braid, was impressed by the butterfly wall and said it was all beautiful. It was.

I opened boxes, stuck my hand in and handed her jewelry.

"For your granddaughter. For you. Please."

I was fearless with generosity even when I was financially wrecked.

That night, the jewelry was worn on stage.

I stood in Yorkville, in a city I did not yet know, and felt something shift.

Not because of celebrity.

Because the universe had sent me a witness.

Day one.
Money in pocket.
Penthouse transformed.
A singer wearing my work.

I thought:

I have landed.

Now, I will call Seamus.

The Illusion of Control

I gave myself a few days before calling him.

In the penthouse bathroom, under lights designed to flatter delusion, I stood in front of the mirror and asked myself:

Do I cry?

Or do I applaud?

Who does this?

Flood.
Financial cliff.
Military-precision relocation.
Penthouse in Yorkville.
Celebrity's grandmother on day one.

It sounds fabricated.

It wasn't.

I had photographs. Contracts. Wire confirmations. Ash from burned pictures still under my nails.

I had always lived like this.

Before "manifesting" had a hashtag.
Before The Secret turned delusion into product.

I believed in bending reality.

Pollyanna optimism spliced with ego and adrenaline. I shook trees. Things fell out. Apartments. Men. Buildings. Opportunities.

Sometimes fruit.

Sometimes snakes.

With Seamus, I had seen Ontario from the back of a Harley. Wind tearing at my hair like I was escaping something. Skinny-dipped in lakes cold enough to reset nerve endings. Sat rink-side at hockey games like I belonged in executive seating. Flown across states on whims that felt cinematic.

I had built buildings.

I had burned buildings.

Metaphorically.

Literally.

But selling handmade jewelry?

That is war.

Love does not scale.
Story does not automatically convert to cash.
Beauty does not pay interest.

I was brilliant at spectacle.

I was reckless at margin.

When I finally called him, my voice was steady.

He brought champagne.

Of course he did.

He always arrived with sparkle, never structure.

We drank it down in the penthouse like conquerors.

Flood?

Irrelevant.

Life on the curb?

Irrelevant.

Credit stretched thin enough to snap?

Irrelevant.

He kissed me like none of it had happened.

And for a moment, it worked.

That is the darkest part.

Addiction has a short memory.

It deletes evidence.

It edits timelines.

It makes a financial cliff feel like a minor inconvenience if the right voice is in the room.

We stood above the city on borrowed altitude, clinking glasses.

He saw the skyline.

I saw the edge.

And I still leaned toward him.

I mistook survival skills for wisdom.

I wasn't bending reality. I was outrunning consequences.

The Key

The superintendent gave me the master key to the penthouses one day for some innocent reason.

I rushed it downstairs.

The key shop on Level One copied it despite the "Do Not Copy" stamp.

Forty-eight floors up in seconds.

I now had access to two vacant penthouses in addition to mine.

Twelve thousand square feet of glass and parquet and marble and fireplaces in downtown Toronto.

It felt like owning a kingdom.

It wasn't mine.

But I could walk through it.

Sometimes, I stood alone in those empty rooms and thought: this is power.

Then, I would go downtown to the CN Tower and try to sell twenty-dollar pins.

Contrast was absurd.

The Shopping Channel

I pitched the cable shopping network again.

I knew I could sell on camera.

I knew my story could translate.

They placed a massive order.

Thousands of pieces.

Best materials.
Canadian-made narrative.
Maple leaf tag stitched into identity.
Beautiful packaging.
My photo on the insert card like proof of authenticity.

I poured money into production.

Staff.
Packaging.
Time.
Belief.

People warned me.

"They can ruin you."

I dismissed it.

I believed in velocity.

I believed in charm.

I believed if I showed up prepared, the world would meet me halfway.

What I did not have was counsel.

I should have had an attorney in my back pocket.

Not hired. Not distant. Not billable by the hour.

The man sleeping in my bed.

He lived in contracts.

He dismantled agreements for sport.

He cross-examined language like it was prey.

He could have read the fine print.

He could have told me where the margins were traps.

He could have said, "Don't accept those terms."

He never offered.

Not once.

He watched me negotiate blind.

He watched me sign.

He watched me flounder.

And I never asked.

That is the part that still burns.

I did not say, "Seamus, read this."

I did not say, "What am I missing?"

I did not say, "Protect me."

I played powerful.

He let me.

On my first show, I made what looked like a cosmetic mistake.

The day before, I had the deluxe facial at Holt Renfrew. I begged the aesthetician to erase every wrinkle. She massaged oil into my skin like polishing marble. I left luminous.

Under studio lights, that oil liquefied.

My face shimmered on the monitor like heat rising from asphalt.

I watched myself melt.

Sales were dismal.

Three chances, they said.

They did not promote me properly.

They did not adjust pricing as promised.

They did not return calls.

They let the inventory stack.

When the contract completed its quiet damage, I was left with thousands of unsold necklaces.

Boxes of hope.

Back in my possession.

That wasn't bad lighting.

That was inexperience meeting predation.

And the man who could have seen it coming stood at a distance and said nothing.

That's how I got blocked.

Not by incompetence.

By silence.

One more nail.

He defended criminals for a living. He did not defend me.

Sugar's

So I did what I always do.

I refused to go quietly.

I improvised.

If the contracts were traps and the penthouse was bleeding money, then the penthouse would produce.

Friday night.

Saturday night.

Doors open.

Sugar's.

Ten-dollar drinks.

A DJ who owed me a favor.

My jewelry draped on dancing girls like moving billboards.

"Buy her that necklace."

"Look at that on you."

"Don't you dare leave without it."

The music hit the glass and bounced back down the walls. Bass vibrating through marble and mirrored ceilings. Bodies packed tight. Champagne sweating on countertops I had nearly lost to the bank.

It was chaotic.

It was partially illegal.

It was electric.

People lined up downstairs like it was Studio 54 with rent due.

And there I was - broke, exhausted, feral - hosting like royalty.

Seamus came.

Of course he did.

He sat in the corner.

Watched.

Did not object.

Did not intervene.

Did not warn me about permits or liquor liability or municipal codes.

The cops did not interfere.

Yorkville is selective about enforcement.

I cooked for the staff between sets. Fed the DJ. Fed the girls. Fed the illusion. Drove across the border for cheaper liquor like a suburban bootlegger in heels.

Two hours of sleep before sunrise.

Wake up.

Clean glitter from grout.

Reset the space.

Do it again.

It was absurd.

It was reckless.

It was a woman refusing to drown politely.

I was selling proximity to spectacle.

Selling adrenaline.

Selling the fantasy that I still controlled the narrative.

The penthouse wasn't a home.

It was a stage.

And if I was going down, I was going down loud.

That's the thing about feral.

It does not ask permission.

It builds clubs in glass towers.

It throws parties on borrowed time.

It dares the city to blink first.

And for a few months, it worked.

Every drink sold was another day the illusion survived."

The Patio

Then one day he said it.

"Fine. You can meet her."

Like he was granting a visa.

I dressed carefully.

Not seductive. Not submissive. Strategic. Clean lines. Composed. I would not be caricatured.

The restaurant patio was downtown. Public. Civilized. The kind of place where reputations sip wine and pretend nothing burns beneath them.

His wife was already seated.

Small. Dark. Older than I had imagined. Not fragile. Contained.

That was the word.

Contained.

He had also invited his friend.

The buffer.

The witness.

The human shield.

I smiled. Warm. Polished. Nonthreatening. I wanted her to see I was not the cliché. Not the predator. Not the destroyer of homes.

His friend leaned back and asked casually, "I never really understood why you moved to Toronto. Your place was amazing."

And I answered honestly.

Because I was tired of performing.

"Because Seamus said he was tired of the commute and might break up with me."

Silence.

The kind that drains color from the table.

Seamus's eyes dropped to his phone.

He took a call.

Stood up.

Walked a few feet away.

Detached.

Then she arrived.

His daughter.

Early twenties. Tiny. Beautiful. Dark Lebanese features like her mother's but with her face red and blazing like something had just detonated inside her.

She didn't sit.

She didn't hesitate.

She stepped directly into my space.

"You whore. Why are you fucking my father?"

The patio froze.

Forks midair. Glasses suspended. Conversations amputated.

I felt every eye.

I did not flinch.

I looked at Seamus.

He laughed.

Not nervous laughter.

Amused.

Delighted.

Like the scene had exceeded expectations.

That was when I understood.

He had told her where we were.

He had engineered it.

He wanted spectacle.

He wanted collision.

He wanted to watch.

Not the flood.

Not the curb.

Not the butt-dial.

This.

This was the moment the architecture became undeniable.

I waited for him to step in.

To say something.

To say I was not a monster.

To say he had lied.

To say he had invited me.

To say I mattered.

He said nothing.

He let his daughter burn me publicly.

He let his wife observe.

He let the restaurant judge.

He stayed neutral.

Which is its own kind of violence.

As we stood to leave, I leaned toward his wife and said quietly, "If you knew me, you would like me."

She smiled.

Not nervous.

Not threatened.

Knowing.

She had the certificate.

The children.

The decades.

She was not competing.

She was anchored.

She got into the car.

They drove away.

An hour later, Seamus showed up at my penthouse.

Laughing.

That was the day I stopped confusing cruelty with complexity.

Replaying it like it was theater.

I opened the door.

I closed it in his face.

He came back the next day.

Sugar's Last Illusion

Be gentle with me.

I will tell it the way it feels when you strip it down to bone.

I wasn't trying to be depraved.

I was trying to win.

I was trying to survive.

I was trying to convert desire into leverage.

If Seamus's native language was sex, I had become fluent.

The penthouse had already morphed into Sugar's.

Music shaking the glass.
Drinks poured heavy.
Ten-dollar magic.

I stood at the door hugging strangers like I was blessing them.

So when someone leaned in one night and said, "You know what this place needs? A wilder version,"

I didn't recoil.

I didn't gasp.

I assessed.

Money.
Seamus.
Attention.
Control.

The categories started bleeding into each other.

I told myself it was empowerment.

Free adults making choices. No shame. No hypocrisy. No small-town morality policing grown bodies.

A hundred dollars at the door for men. Fifty for women. Cheap drinks. Expensive skyline. Food plated like temptation. Music that made people forget the hour.

I told myself I wasn't participating.

I was orchestrating.

I was curating atmosphere.

I was building a room where people could shed their public selves.

I told myself I was in control.

Queen of the castle.

But rogue doesn't announce itself as collapse.

It feels like expansion.

Like you are finally unafraid.

Like you are daring the world to judge you.

Underneath that confidence was something harder.

If Seamus wanted appetite, I would show him abundance.

If he wanted spectacle, I would become the stage.

If he wanted to watch, I would give him something worth watching.

That was the truth I didn't say out loud.

I was not exploring freedom.

I was escalating.

The line between empowerment and exhibition thinned.

The line between orchestration and participation blurred.

The line between control and chaos flickered.

And the most dangerous part?

I liked the power.

Not the bodies.

Not the skin.

The power of the room shifting when I entered.

The power of men paying to step into a space I controlled.

The power of Seamus sitting back, watching me command something he thought he had invented.

That's what you would have believed.

That I was untouchable.

But rogue isn't about confidence.

Rogue is about what happens when you start daring yourself to see how far you can go.

And not caring who gets scorched.

I thought I was commanding the room. I didn't realize I was feeding the fire.

The Room

At first, it was harmless.

Laughter.
Low music.
Lights dimmed just enough to flatter.

My art glowed. Felt butterflies spiraled across the wall. Toronto glittered below like it had been hired as background.

I poured drinks.
I smiled.
I floated.

Seamus was there.

I told myself: this will remind him who I am.

This will make him choose me.

Later, I realized I hadn't seen him in a while.

Then someone said it casually, almost kindly:

"Oh, he's upstairs."

My bedroom.

I walked up slowly.

Still composed.

Still the hostess.

When I opened the door, I did not enter fantasy.

I entered rupture.

My Ralph Lauren bedspread had been dragged off the bed and spread across the floor like a staging ground. Two bodies on it. Facing the windows. Facing the skyline I had paid for.

He wasn't with me.

He wasn't looking for me.

He wasn't restrained.

He was doing something he had always refused me.

Something he had dismissed.
Mocked.
Drawn a line around.

He had said it was beneath him.

He had called it degrading.

He had positioned himself as principled.

And there he was.

Eager.

Fully engaged.

With a 20-year-old stunning young girl who had a body like a ballerina. So flawless and luminous that rooms tilted toward her when she entered.

The prize.

And he looked alive.

That was the split.

Not that it was a sex party.

I had sanctioned chaos.

Not that he was with someone else.

I had invited appetite.

It was the aliveness.

The hunger.

The absence of hesitation.

He had rationed himself with me.

Measured.

Contained.

Suddenly, there was no containment.

And it was happening on my floor. On my blanket. In the penthouse I had financed.

I had done everything he asked sexually.

Escalated.

Over-delivered.

Proved myself fearless.

He demurred.

He deflected.

He postponed.

Now he was performing something he had told me he would never do.

The hypocrisy was not subtle.

It was surgical.

That was the humiliation.

That was the blade.

It wasn't about bodies.

It was about realization.

I had mistaken his boundaries for morality.

They were preferences.

And I had never been the preference.

That is when the rabid part began.

Not screaming.

Not throwing things.

Something inside me snapped its leash.

That was the moment love turned feral.

The Turn

I froze for half a second.

Not disbelief.

System overload.

My brain trying to reconcile the skyline, the music downstairs, the butterflies on the wall, the contract I had signed with myself that this was control.

Then my body reacted.

Cold first.

A flash freeze that ran from my scalp to my spine.

Then heat.

Then something volcanic and ancient that did not ask permission.

I crossed the room before thought could intervene.

My nails dragged up his back - from the base of him to the back of his neck - raking skin hard enough to leave memory. He didn't even register I was there until my fist closed in his hair.

Not elegant.

Not composed.

Not strategic.

Animal.

The leash snapped.

"I cannot believe you're doing that."

My voice didn't sound like mine.

Thirty minutes earlier, I had declared freedom. No shame. No rules.

But I had always carried one clause I never said aloud.

Not him.

Not like this.

Not on my blanket.

He stood up.

Fully exposed.

And when he looked at me, there was no guilt.

No embarrassment.

No flicker of remorse.

There was hate.

Cold.

Clinical.

As if I had violated something sacred by interrupting.

That was new.

That was the moment the room shifted from chaos to war.

He dressed in under a minute.

Efficient.

Detached.

Already recalibrating.

He moved toward the back door that led to the private elevator.

He fled.

Not from danger.

From accountability.

I followed.

Barefoot.

Heart slamming against bone.

Down the hallway, past art I had curated, past walls I had painted, through a space I had paid for.

I wasn't chasing a lover.

I was chasing the truth.

The elevator doors slid closed between us like a guillotine.

I stood there shaking.

Not crying.

Shaking.

Because rage is clarifying.

In that split second, something irreversible crystallized.

He didn't hate me because I interrupted sex.

He hated me because I had seen him.

Unmasked.

Uncontained.

Unfaithful not just in body, but in narrative.

And once you see that, you cannot be managed the same way again.

That was the real explosion.

Not the scratching.

Not the shouting.

The realization that I had just stepped outside the box he had built for me.

And he did not forgive that.

That was the night I stopped being obsessed and started being dangerous.

The Elevator

I caught my reflection in the mirrored hallway.

Braless.
Silver Whiting & Davis metal halter top catching every shard of light.
White and silver kitten heels.
Soft blue silk sari skirt stitched with tiny silver glass beads.

I looked like disco royalty mid-collapse.

Glamour unraveling in real time.

I lunged into the elevator just as the doors began to seal. Slipped inside like a shadow he couldn't shake. It wasn't until he turned toward the doors that he saw me standing there.

Forty-eight floors.

The descent felt endless.

I screamed the entire way down.

Not cute.
Not theatrical.
Not clever.

From the diaphragm.
From the gut.

From the place that understood, finally, what had just happened.

The sound ricocheted off chrome and mirrored panels. It didn't belong in a penthouse. It belonged in a field somewhere, feral and uncontained.

"You never gave me that!"

That was the truth beneath the spectacle.

Not jealousy.

Not prudishness.

Not wounded ego.

You never gave me that.

I had given him everything.

I built buildings for him.

Moved cities for him.

Lit money on fire for him.

Opened my bed, my home, my name, my future.

I escalated until there was nothing left to escalate.

And he rationed himself to me.

Measured affection.
Measured risk.
Measured hunger.

But not to her.

There was no rationing there.

That's the betrayal.

Not the bodies.

The disparity.

The deliberate withholding.

The knowledge that the limit had never been moral.

It had been mc.

The elevator kept dropping.

Forty-eight floors of realization.

And when the doors opened, something inside me had already burned down.

Not love.

Illusion.

The limit was never the act. The limit was me.

The Street

He ran.

I chased.

Shoes flying.

One heel skidding across marble. The other snapping off somewhere near the concierge desk.

Bare feet hitting Toronto pavement like I'd been exiled from my own kingdom.

I was no longer Sugar.

No longer hostess. No longer strategist. No longer queen of altitude.

I was a wound.

He cut down side streets.

I followed.

Forty-eight floors of rage still ringing in my ears.

He ducked into doorways, slipped around corners like he'd done it a thousand times before.

Of course he had.

He had lived in pursuit and evasion for decades.

This was just another scene to him.

To me, it was blood.

I hunted him.

Not gracefully.

Hair wild. Metal halter flashing under streetlights like armor in a war I didn't train for.

People stared.

Cabs slowed.

Patio diners froze mid-bite.

Mascara probably streaking.

Breath tearing at my ribs.

My voice cracked from screaming his name, from screaming the truth, from screaming the realization that I had just been publicly erased in my own city.

He didn't turn back.

He didn't try to calm me.

He didn't try to gather me.

He ran.

Then a taxi.

Yellow blur.

Door flung open.

He slid inside like an escape artist.

I reached it just as it slammed shut.

I threw a shoe.

Hard.

It hit metal with a sharp, useless crack.

The cab pulled away.

Red taillights shrinking.

And just like that…

Gone.

I stood there.

Breathing like I had outrun a fire.

Hair feral.

Silver top catching the light.

Barefoot on Yorkville concrete.

Penthouse queen turned sidewalk spectacle.

People whispering.

Phones maybe raised.

The skyline still glittering above as if nothing had happened.

That was the image.

Not the glamour.

Not the club.

Not the screenplay.

A woman who had climbed to the sky and come crashing down in kitten heels.

And the worst part?

I wasn't embarrassed.

I was awake.

That was the night the city saw me feral and I stopped caring who was watching.

The Truth

I thought I lost everything that night.

I didn't.

What I lost was fantasy.

The fantasy that sex could purchase loyalty.

The fantasy that spectacle could intimidate him into choosing me.

The fantasy that scale - penthouses, clubs, contracts, altitude - could outmuscle a marriage certificate, children, and decades of shared infrastructure.

I lost the belief that intensity equals leverage.

That was the real casualty.

But I didn't lose myself.

Not yet.

I went back upstairs.

Alone.

The penthouse still humming with bass from downstairs. The skyline still glittering like it had no stake in my humiliation.

I still had the empire of glass.

And even with mascara drying stiff on my face, even with the image of him on my floor burned into my skull, I was calculating.

That's the part that unsettles me now.

Not the screaming.

Not the shoe thrown at a taxi.

The math.

Even after that exposure.

Even after seeing him fully unmasked.

Even after understanding, with surgical clarity, that I had never been the priority.

I still believed I could pivot.

I still believed I could win.

That's addiction.

Not to sex.

Not to him.

To the game.

I told myself it wasn't over.

I wasn't finished.

The real question isn't what he did that night.

The real question is this:

Why did I stay in motion after the truth was undeniable?

Did I finally see him clearly?

Or did I see the board more clearly?

Because the woman who chased him barefoot through Yorkville wasn't hysterical.

She was detonated.

And detonation rearranges structure.

Something cracked that night.

Not my pride.

My architecture.

And once you understand that you've been competing in a game designed for you to lose, you don't return to innocence.

You either walk away.

Or you go rogue.

Rogue Sugar

A friend stayed with me that night.

She slept in my bed and held me while I came apart in controlled silence.

I didn't sleep.

I lay awake staring at the ceiling I had once thought meant victory. Forty-eight floors above consequence.

In the morning, there was a festival below the penthouse. Corn roasting. Music. Children sticky with sugar. Couples holding hands like the world was stable.

I walked through it hollowed out.

My friend laced her fingers through mine. We must have looked like a couple. It felt grounding to have a pulse next to mine. I needed something solid. Something not shifting.

Toronto had once felt like destiny.

Now it felt like a stage set after the actors had left.

Something had hardened inside me overnight.

Not sadness.

Steel.

Later, after she left, I called him.

"I want to talk."

I went to his apartment. He wouldn't buzz me in.

So I followed a pizza delivery through the door and went upstairs.

I refused to leave.

He finally opened it.

On the kitchen counter was his service weapon.

That's how he saw me now.

A threat.

His friend quietly slid the gun farther away from where I stood.

I looked at it.

"I'm not going to touch that," I said. "I'm not here to kill you. I'm here to tell you what a bastard you are."

Then I walked out.

That should have been the end.

It wasn't.

Ugly texts. Silence. Then the Olympic hockey game.

I invited him over.

Come watch it with me.

I told myself we'd keep it light. Cook. Sit. Be normal. Pretend we were salvageable.

He hesitated. Tried to back out.

Then said yes.

He didn't show.

I drove to his apartment.

No car.

I pulled tax records. Found his wife's address.

Around the corner.

I drove there. Parked. Waited.

His car in the driveway.

Children's cars too.

He was inside with them. Watching the game. Playing husband.

I called.

No answer.

Again.

Again.

Finally, he picked up.

"Why are you calling?"

"It must have been a butt dial," I said.

Silence.

"Don't call me again."

"You're a bastard."

Click.

The next day, one of his lawyer friends served me papers.

Do not contact.

Or else.

A court order.

That should have ended it.

It didn't.

You don't shut off something that pushed you to the edge of yourself with paperwork.

A month later, I called from a pay phone.

He answered.

"Do you miss me?"

"Yes," he said. "I miss you."

Still there.

Still hooked into the bloodstream.

We met outside.

I said mi culpa.

It wasn't only him.

It was two addicts circling voltage.

Then I told him my plan.

"I'm loading jewelry into my car and driving across Canada. Selling to stores. Sleeping in the backseat if I have to."

He looked unimpressed.

Just another Sugar spectacle.

I did it anyway.

I needed road.

Distance.

Air that didn't carry his name.

I drove Highway 1 to its end.

Sold jewelry from the trunk.

Met shop owners in towns so small they blinked when I arrived.

What I sold paid for gas and food.

Sometimes I slept in the car.

Sometimes cheap motels.

Always put together. Lipstick on. Earrings gleaming. Selling beauty while stitched together with willpower.

I wrote every night from my pallet in the backseat. Facebook before everyone curated their lives. Raw dispatches from the edge.

People followed.

No one knew I was outrunning humiliation.

I dipped into the States. Made a wide loop. Knocked on doors. Visited rock stores. Tried to sell to Harley Davidson. Karen Davidson remembered me from Toronto parties.

Money was tight.

Not broke.

Just bruised.

That month saved me.

I picked up a man in a bar once.

Smoked something I shouldn't have.

Laughed too loud.

Reminded myself I was alive.

It wasn't about sex.

It was about agency.

When I came back to Toronto, I saw Seamus a few times.

But something had thinned.

The building board discovered Sugar's Club. Illegal liquor runs. After-hours chaos.

They gave me a choice.

Be voted out.

Or move downstairs into a smaller unit.

Month to month.

I moved.

Smaller. Lower. Quieter.

Then I bought a cottage on Rice Lake.

Not romance.

Utility.

Half my things needed a place.

Half my life needed a project.

The floors weren't level. Fireplace unfinished. Walls raw. Windows tired. Weeds everywhere.

Good.

It kept my hands busy.

Away from him.

Then the Queen came to town.

I had been supplying government shops. Given pieces to Prince Charles and Camilla before. I met the Queen.

Back in the spotlight.

Of course, he saw it on television.

He called.

We slid toward each other briefly.

But it wasn't the same.

I could feel it.

The tether fraying.

At some point, the tug came.

Leave.

Toronto had too many ghosts.

Texas had more people than all of Canada.

Bigger market.

Different air.

Fewer memories with his fingerprints on them.

So I left.

Again.

Not because I was broken.

Because I was done orbiting a man who thrived on compartmentalizing women.

That's Rogue Sugar.

Not hysterical.

Not destroyed.

Rebuilt.

On the road.

On instinct.

On fire.

Swearing-In

By then, I was already practicing exit.

You don't leave in a single motion.
You rehearse it.
You begin standing differently in rooms.

I went to Waterloo to say goodbye to friends I knew I would miss in a way that doesn't fade.

It felt ceremonial.

My best friend's husband had gone to law school with Seamus. They had opposed each other in court. We had shared a few dinners together. It felt civilized. Almost normal.

He asked casually, "Where's Seamus?"

"He can't come," I said. "He has to attend a judge's swearing-in. It's his baby momma."

David went pale.

Not theatrical pale.

Drained.

"You mean Taylor?" he asked.

"Yes."

He sat down slowly, like the floor had shifted.

For years, he had carried a private story inside himself. A child he thought might be his. An affair he had buried. A question that never stopped humming.

She had kept the father secret.

He had done the math in silence.

Turns out the math was wrong.

The affair had been real.

But the child wasn't his.

It was Seamus's.

Of course it was.

They had graduated together. Young attorneys. Ambition sharp and hot. Seamus married with three children. The optics alone required silence.

His wife had absorbed the child into the marriage.

A blessing, publicly.

A containment strategy, privately.

David recalculated his entire past in one breath.

Relief is not fireworks.

Relief is air returning to lungs you didn't know were constricted.

He admitted the affair in that moment. To me. To his wife. To himself.

A confession braided to exoneration.

His wife stood there.

I stood there.

Everyone adjusting the ledger in real time.

No screaming.

No glass breaking.

Just the sound of a narrative collapsing.

The judge took her oath.

The courtroom applauded.

And a man who had carried a phantom child for years finally set it down.

Seamus had fathered another secret.

Another compartment.

Another life folded into the architecture of his marriage.

And I remember thinking—

Of course he could build two futures at once.

He had been building three.

The Long Goodbye

As my days filled with logistics and exit strategies, Seamus called.

"Hockey game," he said.

Less than two weeks before I was leaving the country.

He picked me up in a new red BMW convertible.

New.

I had a small lamp for him. A tiny table. A wooden box I had made by hand because he loved the way I built things.

I brought him pieces of myself.

He brought nothing.

After parking, he took me upstairs to a condo in the Maple Leafs' sports complex. Steps from the rink.

He had lived there for a year.

A year.

I had never been invited. Never told.

It was sleek. Polished. Bachelor-perfect. Views that mirrored my penthouse. A bathroom that held small feminine artifacts I pretended not to see.

A sweater on a chair.

"Is that yours?" I asked lightly.

"It's my daughter's."

Some lies do not detonate.

They dissolve into the air and settle on your skin.

We watched the game from his box seats.

Crowds roaring. Lights blazing. Everything loud and alive.

I couldn't concentrate.

All I could think was: you built another life without me.

I wanted the buzzer to sound. I wanted to leave with him. I wanted something that felt like the last time.

Instead, he drove me home and let me out.

I cried in the passenger seat.

He said he would see me once more.

Rice Lake

He came to the cottage the weekend before I left.

The lake was still. Gray and endless.

We sat near the water like people who had already said goodbye in their heads.

There had been so many versions of us.

Motorcycle summers. Penthouse nights. Courtroom stories. Chaos. Fire.

Now, there was just quiet.

Watching David surrender a story he had carried for years had taught me something.

We suffer under narratives we defend long after they stop serving us.

Seamus and I didn't need one more explosion.

We needed truth.

We didn't have sex.

That was the strangest mercy.

We held each other instead.

Laughed at how unhinged we had been. How dramatic. How combustible.

We said we would never forget each other.

We meant it.

When he drove away, I waited until his car cleared the bend in the road.

Then I ran.

Behind the cottage. Out of sight.

I ran like something had been ripped out of my chest.

I screamed, "Please don't leave. Please don't leave."

No one heard me but the trees.

He didn't come back.

I didn't call.

That was the real ending.

TEXAS

Austin

Somewhere south on I-35, half awake in the truck cab, I saw a sign:

Free movies. Hot showers.

That was enough.

I pulled in.

Everything I owned sat in that parking lot. I took a room facing the truck so I could watch it through the blinds.

I turned on the TV.

Whip It was playing.

Roller derby girls. Bruised knees. Girls refusing to stay small.

The first line I heard when I turned it on was about Austin being where you're supposed to be.

I was too tired to argue with omens.

I took the shower.

Slept flat.

Kept driving.

Austin did not care who I had been.

No one knew Seamus.

No one knew the Sugar Factory.

No one knew my penthouse or my club or my humiliation.

There is something brutal about anonymity after living at altitude.

I found a building on Koenig Lane. Busy road. Beige. Tired. Forgettable.

Perfect.

I lived and worked there. No marble. No skyline. No glass empire.

Just heat.

Three straight months of 100-degree weather with no rain.

I painted the exterior myself. Giant bouncing dots. Glitter in the paint. Refused to let beige win.

I stapled tiger-patterned towels onto Craigslist chairs because fabric was too expensive.

I painted bare branches gold, wired them with tiny lights, hung crystals down the hallway so it shimmered at night.

I made beauty out of leftovers.

Again.

I placed Craigslist ads for photographers to use my jewelry.

I hustled.

The AC ran constantly because no one wants to shop in a furnace. The electric bill bit hard. Customers stayed in their cars. I survived. I did not thrive.

I made friends.

Got press.

Built something small and strange and mine.

But it was different now.

No Seamus orbiting it.

No man watching from a leather chair.

No audience to impress.

Just me and heat and invoices.

I went back to Ottawa once to gift Prince William and Princess Kate a crown. Cameras. Headlines. Global news.

Seamus saw it.

He called.

We laughed.

But I did not ask to see him.

That was new.

I went to Rice Lake to prepare the cottage for sale and found the friend who had once held my hand had used it as her private escape.

Trash left behind. Rotting food. Careless damage.

People love what you build. Few respect what it cost you.

I cleaned it.

Sold it.

Closed that door.

And somewhere in the middle of Koenig heat and mounting bills, I had a revelation.

Twelve years of being an artist.

Handmade jewelry is poetry.

It is not scalable income.

Love does not convert automatically to profit.

Story does not pay electric bills.

I had chased spectacle.

Then survival.

Now I needed stability.

So I took the proceeds from selling Rice Lake and enrolled in an advanced IT program at the University of Texas.

Not glamorous.

Not glittered.

Strategic.

It was the first decision in years that was not about a man.

Not about proving something.

Not about winning.

It was about structure.

I had finally chosen structure.

And Then

And Then

A few years later, I nearly died.

Complications from a surgery. Damage no one had predicted. My body shutting down in slow, clinical increments.

There was a moment - and I do not care who believes this - when I watched myself from above.

Turquoise.

That was the color.

My soul lifting, unbothered by invoices or men or unfinished conversations.

Then I came back.

Bruised. Altered. Alive.

Someone told him.

Maybe a mutual friend. Maybe someone saw my Facebook post about seeing that turquoise light and panicked. News travels strangely.

My phone rang.

His name lit the screen.

My body froze before my mind did.

I almost didn't answer.

But curiosity is a reflex I have always struggled to kill.

"Hello?"

His voice.

Same cadence. Same effortless authority.

"I love you," he said. "Stay here. You're needed."

Needed.

Not cherished.

Not chosen.

Needed.

He bantered lightly, like we were picking up mid-sentence from some suspended summer. I heard that laugh. The one that used to disarm rooms.

And I felt sick.

Not fluttering.

Not weak.

Ill.

Because suddenly I could see it clearly: even death would have been folded into his architecture. Another compartment. Another narrative he could step into when it suited him.

I said, "I died. I came back. I'll be fine."

There was a pause.

"But please don't call me again."

And I hung up.

No chase.

No scream.

No pay phone.

Just silence.

I sat there shaking.

Not because I wanted him.

Because I didn't.

That was the shock.

I was proud of myself in a way that felt quiet and adult.

I did not open the drawers where I had stored him.

The mental ones.

The sensory ones.

The ones with the lake water and the motorcycle exhaust and the penthouse lights.

I left them closed.

Near-death rearranges scale.

When you see turquoise and then return to a body that barely works, you stop mistaking intensity for destiny.

He was not destiny.

He was a lesson in compartmentalized power.

I survived him.

Then I survived my own body.

That felt like the real graduation.

And Then Once More

Years Later

Years passed.

Then a woman began liking my Facebook posts.

I didn't know her.

At first, it felt harmless. A stranger drifting through my digital life. But her comments were slightly off. Familiar in a way that made my skin prickle.

So I looked at her profile.

Toronto.

Mutual connections.

Seamus's friends.

I began commenting back. Lightly. Casually. We became online "friends."

Soon she messaged me.

Then asked if she could call.

I said yes.

At first, she told me about herself. Asked polite questions about my life. The usual circling.

Then she dropped it.

While I was with Seamus, she had been living in his condo.

Moved in when he first bought it.

Helped him furnish it.

The condo I had seen once.

The one with the sweater on the chair.

The feminine artifacts in the bathroom.

Her.

She told me he had given her his computer passwords to fix something once. He never changed them.

She read my emails.

My texts.

She knew everything I had written.

She said he told her all about me. That they laughed at my photos. My blonde hair. My big breasts. That she was dark and nearly flat-chested. That we were opposites.

Like his wife.

She rode on the back of his motorcycle all over Ontario.

He introduced her to his friends.

She said she thought she was special.

Then she said something else.

While I was fighting for him - penthouses, parties, road trips, spectacle - she was behind the curtain.

And the wife was in front of it.

Three narratives.

Three women.

One man.

She admitted she became obsessive too.

Showed up at the rink when he was with his family.

Flew to Nantucket to hover near him during a vacation.

He eventually threw her out.

Restraining order.

Devastation.

Now she was spiraling.

She wanted my advice.

How to get him back.

I listened.

Calm.

Detached.

I realized something that no longer hurt.

I was never competing with one woman.

I was competing with a system.

He compartmentalized intimacy the way other men compartmentalize files.

Each woman served a function.

Wife: structure.

Me: spectacle.

Her: access.

And when one destabilized, another filled the space.

He was very good at lying.

He was better at maintaining parallel worlds.

As far as I know, he still has his wife.

Good for him.

Good for her.

I hope she reads this.

Because this was never a love triangle.

It was architecture.

And I finally walked out of the building.

Some stories don't end.

You just stop volunteering to be in them.

THE END

About the Author

Sugar Gay Isber McMillan is an artist, entrepreneur and writer whose work spans jewelry design, storytelling and reinvention.

A sixth-generation Texan with a Canadian passport, she has lived and built businesses on both sides of the border. She is best known for creating bold, narrative-driven jewelry and immersive creative spaces that blend art, spectacle and personal myth. Her work has appeared in media across North America and has been gifted to members of the British Royal Family.

Her creative career has included founding multiple versions of The Sugar Factory, teaching, public speaking and designing for private clients and public figures. She later pivoted into advanced technology studies at the University of Texas, proving that reinvention is not an event but a practice.

This book reflects her personal experiences and perspective. Certain names, identifying details and circumstances have been changed for privacy.

She lives in Texas, where she continues to write, design and build. And is happily married to a great man.

www.ingramcontent.com/pod-product-compliance
Lightning Source LLC
LaVergne TN
LVHW081317110826
845149LV00006B/1528

* 9 7 8 1 9 6 7 9 7 3 8 7 3 *